AN AVALON ROMANCE

PITTER PATTER
Cathy Liggett

Two events happen within days of each other to make Samantha Stevenson's heart go pitter patter. The first is when Blake Dawson, a handsome lawyer with an irresistible British accent, drops unexpectedly into her life. The second is when a precious baby girl is abandoned on her doorstep.

Too bad Sam is already engaged to Prescott Sterling IV, a controlling man who has no time for unexpected things . . . or unforeseen additions to his prestigious family. Too bad she doesn't want to give up Emma, the new baby girl in her life.

Sam knows her heart is finally leading her to the right people to love; indeed her makeshift family is opening her heart to the possibilities of love. Surely something that feels so right can't be wrong?

As weeks go by, Sam discovers the one-of-a-kind joy of loving a child, as well as an unexpected passion for a certain handsome Brit. As that circle of love is tested by the return of the baby's biological parents, and the wrath of her ex-fiance's mother, Sam learns that she must choose her future, and the one man who can make her heart go pitter patter.

PITTER PATTER

•

Cathy Liggett

AVALON BOOKS
NEW YORK

PRINTED IN THE UNITED STATES OF AMERICA
ON ACID-FREE PAPER
BY HADDON CRAFTSMEN, BLOOMSBURG, PENNSYLVANIA

To Mark, Kelly, and Michael.
Nothing would have meaning
without you.

Love you!

My utmost thanks to Shelley Sabga, Heather Webber, Hilda Lindner Knepp, Julie Stone, Nancy Bentz, and Jay Clark for their continued encouragement, wisdom, and sweet way of prodding. I'm blessed to have you as my support team and most of all as my friends.

Special thanks too, to Abby Holcomb, for giving me this first chance. Your name will be etched in my memory.

Mom and Dad . . . I couldn't write about love if I hadn't been shown it.

Chapter One

"A guy as sweet as me could positively melt out there," the dark-haired man in the billowy trench coat announced as he stepped into Chausseures Shoe Boutique.

At the commotion, Sam glanced up momentarily from the basic white pump she held. She watched the man stomp his soaked Italian loafers on the floor mat, and heard the blustery, rain-swept wind blow the door to a clamorous close behind him.

His noisy entrance was startling. His British accent staggering. Its alluring effect was practically visible to the naked eye. Like sprinkles of golden fairy dust, it drifted from one female patron to the next, instantly charming them, one by one. Some women tittered back at him. One older woman batted her eyes demurely like a starlet from an old-time movie. Some smiled sweetly . . . others langourously.

Shaking loose the raindrops from his collar, he was seemingly unaware that he had just cast a spell on every female shopper in the shoe boutique. And all within two seconds flat.

Well, on every female except for Sam, who couldn't help but muse to herself about the fate of the brassy Englishman.

Wonder how Uncle Dominic will handle this one? She stood back and looked on with amused curiosity.

After all, the Brit's rumbling entrance had totally disrupted Chausseures' typically quiet ambience. Surely Uncle Dominic would politely admonish the man, take him aside and quietly speak to him.

She watched as her uncle, Dominic Barnaclo, looking every bit the debonair proprietor with his peppered moustache and perfectly knotted tie, approached the Brit. But instead of squelching the Englishman, he thrust his arms wide open and welcomed him enthusiastically.

"B.D.!" Uncle Dom cried out, also raising his voice well past the normal "boutique decibel" range. "It's you!"

"D.B.!" The man answered in kind. "Indeed it is."

Sam dropped her jaw and nearly the linen pump as well, watching as the two men hugged warmly, looking as familiar as father and son. Delighting in their reunion, they performed a convoluted secret handshake of sorts, and laughed jovially when Uncle Dominic couldn't get his part right.

"It's been a long time," she heard her uncle say.

"Truly, sir," B.D. answered him, grinning openly. "My father sends his very best, of course. And my mother sends a kiss—though I'll refrain from delivering that particular sentiment."

Uncle Dom chuckled at that, clasped the younger man

on the shoulder and led him around the store, pointing out certain inventory while exchanging tidbits of news.

Funny . . . Sam thought *. . . Uncle Dom never seems even a smidgen that pleased to see Prescott.*

Prescott Sterling. Her fiancé. The man she'd hoped her Aunt Maria and Uncle Dom would embrace, being that they were childless and had no other nieces or nephews. And if not for her aunt and uncle, Sam had hoped it for herself. Ever since her mother and father had separated and relocated to opposite sides of the country, Aunt Maria and Uncle Dom had become like surrogate parents to her.

But her aunt—and especially her Uncle Dom—never seemed to warm to Prescott for some reason. Sam tried to explain to them that it wasn't Prescott's fault he was a fourth generation Sterling and heir to a multi-million dollar fortune. Anyone growing up with five-course meals, a butler, and a nanny might seem a little stiff, a little too formal, and unbending at times, right?

No, Prescott certainly wasn't like this B.D. fellow whom her uncle seemed so delighted to see.

Whereas Prescott was more quiet and reserved, the Englishman appeared full of life. Totally animated, his hands moving, his eyes expressive as he talked with Uncle Dom. And though his dark suit topped off by a khaki trench coat gave him the air of a gentleman with a crisp and cool demeanor, the way he sifted his fingers through his crop of thick, wavy hair had a casual, boyish sort of appeal to it.

At the thought, Prescott's diamond-clustered engagement ring, a Sterling family heirloom, weighed heavy on her finger. She felt guilty for making such comparisons between the two men.

But maybe that's what jittery brides-to-be tend to do, Sam thought, seeking to ease her conscience. Anyway, it didn't mean anything, did it? It was normal. A mere observation, she reassured herself as she turned her gaze from the boisterous Brit and attempted to concentrate on the white heel once again. That is, until she caught the tail end of her uncle's sentence.

"—must meet my niece."

Her eyes shot open wide. Her heart leaped in her chest as Uncle Dom guided "B.D." over to where she was standing at the display of traditional linen pumps.

Even from across the store, something about the Englishman put her survival instincts on high alert. Probably the way he'd successfully disarmed every female in the store simply with a flash of his smile and an off-handed, witty comment. But now he was coming within striking distance. And even nearer still as her uncle urged the Englishman toward her with a gentle hand at his back.

"B.D.," her uncle introduced the pair, his face beaming, "this is Samantha Stevenson, my niece."

Then, as if the two adults needed assistance, her uncle deftly switched positions, giving Sam a gentle, but noticeable, nudge closer to B.D. "Samantha, this is Blake Dawson, also known as B.D."

The Englishman held out his hand. Sam thought twice about taking it. Talk about survival instincts! Up close, the Brit's charm was undeniably palpable. Still crisp and cool on the outside, but so much more touchable. Especially with that pair of dimples dotting his tapered cheeks when he smiled. And that pair of warm green-gold eyes flickering at her roguishly, playfully. The slightest, sweetest lines tweaked at their edges. *So he laughed a lot, huh?*

She drew a deep breath, feeling the intensity of his eyes on her . . . and couldn't help but feel the eyes of the other women in the store watching her every move as well.

"Sam," she told him, expelling the in-drawn breath. She politely took his hand.

"Blake," he replied, a half-smile still playing on his lips. He squeezed her hand gently, as if by revealing their preferred names, they'd sealed a pact between themselves.

His clasp was warm to the touch; his direct gaze enough to melt away any female's defenses. Luckily, her uncle spoke up just then, breaking the Englishman's spell.

"Will you two excuse me for a moment?" He pointed toward a Chippendale desk at the front of the shop where a woman was standing with a return package. Obviously she'd just entered the store and had missed out on Blake's grandiose entrance. She appeared impatient to do her business and leave, unlike the other women in the store whose eyes and ears lingered on Sam and Blake.

"So, Sam." Blake tilted his chestnut brow, looking at her uncertainly. "How long have you been Dominic's niece?" he asked seriously.

She barely managed to suppress a giggle. "Excuse me?"

"Er—" he shifted on his feet and recomposed himself. "What I meant to say was, my family has known your aunt and uncle since the beginning of time—well, at least since the beginning of my time." He laid a well-groomed hand on his chest. "How is it that I've never heard of you?"

"Oh, well . . ." She felt her face color slightly. As a

Cathy Liggett

director of the Somersby Children's Services Agency, she dealt with broken homes on a daily basis, removing neglected children from abusive situations, bringing unwanted babies and hand-picked parents together.

But still . . . silly as it seemed, even as an adult, her own parents' separation wasn't something she had dealt with so easily. Maybe because they'd been married for twenty-four years before they parted ways. And now even two years later she still hadn't completely gotten over the shock of it. Though lately she'd been feeling that the hurt was finally fading . . . and so were her hopes that her mom and dad would ever get back together again.

"About the time I found a job back home in Somersby, my parents were ready to move away," she said vaguely, lifting her shoulder with a blithe indifference she didn't really feel. "Uncle Dominic and Aunt Maria sort of became my adoptive parents."

"Well, I don't know who's luckier then." His words seemed sincere, a gleam of interest shining in his eyes. An unwelcome blush crept to her cheeks.

"Yes, they're great people," she agreed softly, placing the shoe back on its slanted clear plastic display. Distracted by the Englishman and the sudden jumble of emotions swirling about inside of her, there was no way she'd be making any decisions about wedding shoes today.

Seeing her return the shoe to its resting place, Blake leaned toward her, bending his nearly six-foot frame down to hers. His arms linked comfortably behind his back, he spoke in a hushed, confidential tone. "Dreadful, aren't they?"

She could barely make out the word. "Dreadful?" she repeated, confused.

He nodded discreetly at the display of linen pumps. "A classic style, true, but still . . ." He grimaced with exaggerated sourness. "By the standards of today's woman, I'd think they'd be considered rather—"

He leaned over closer this time, his lips falling near to her ear, raising the fine hairs on her neck on end.

"—drab."

He finished the sentence and for a moment she had no idea what he was referring to. The heat of his breath tingled . . . tickled. So close, the slight scent of him, musk and male, dizzied . . . disturbed her senses.

Oh, the shoes! She remembered as he kept on talking.

"Now, take this . . ." He picked up another dressy pump from a display table to the right, continuing his monologue. "Ah, yes. This looks like something you'd much prefer." He held the ebony shoe at eye level and turned it in his hand. "Am I right? Style. Lightness. Flair. Enough to set a pair of lovely feet to music." He swept a hand across it. "And all in indubitably good taste."

She couldn't believe it. Before her final destination at the table of basic linen pumps, she was stopped dead by the exact shoe he was holding. The pitch of the heel. The strappy design. Its mere name, *Twilight Tango*, had called out to her. Beckoned her. Seemed like a perfect fit.

But three little words had turned her attention away from the trendy breathtaking heels to the display of traditional, conservative one and one half-inch pumps. And the words weren't "Marked for Clearance." But rather "Genevieve Elizabeth Sterling"—Prescott's domineering mother.

The Sterling matriarch had the bluest blood this side of the Ohio River—actually make that the Mississippi. The woman never let anyone forget how she'd managed to raise two children while maintaining the family's assets after her husband passed away suddenly. All of which made her the ultimate authority on everything—from widgets to weddings—and the correct shoes to be worn at such occasions.

"I do, um—I do like to dance," she confessed shyly.

Why had she said that? No one danced any more. He was just being colorful, continental—while she sounded totally corny. She could feel the redness creep into her cheeks. Self-conscious, she readily shifted the conversation back to him.

"You seem to know a lot about women's taste in shoes," she prompted.

She could still sense the other women glaring at her, their stares along with Blake's intense eyes making her feel overheated in her raincoat.

"Actually," he rubbed his chin thoughtfully, "I prefer to think I know a great deal about women. Of course," he paused to wink at her, his eyes twinkling teasingly, "it *is* a study that I've enjoyed dabbling in over the years."

At that, she rolled her eyes, but couldn't contain her smile. A smile revealing he'd captured her attention, making her a captivated audience of one. It was all he needed to continue.

"In fact," he cocked his head and conjured up a faraway, theatrical gaze, "it all started out innocently enough with Melinda Briggs."

"Dear Melinda," he mused in remembrance. "Melin and I were at the seasoned age of six when we met. I was quite intrigued with her, growing up in a house full of male siblings as I had. Whenever the chance came along to play with my friend of the opposite sex, I grabbed it." He chuckled delightedly. "But the dear girl was slightly on the klutzy side. Not too coordinated, that one. She was forever getting nicked and knocked about. Of course, being the chivalrous lad I was, I'd always come to her rescue." His eyes narrowed engagingly as he asked, "And do you know what I discovered made her feel better?"

"I'm almost afraid to ask." She wagged her head at him, amused but skeptical of the roguish answer she'd receive.

His index finger waved in the air as definitively as if he were addressing Parliament. "Chocolate," he answered her.

"Excuse me?" She chuckled, inclining her head to meet his gaze.

"The fact of the matter was," he told her without blinking, "I'd give Melin candies, ice creams, all sort of things to make her 'get well' as it were." He made quotation marks with his hands. "But of everything, every time, she'd always prefer the chocolate items I offered. Ding!" He pointed to his head of dark hair. "That was my first clue into the hearts of women."

"I see," Sam replied, the easygoing conversation making her mouth curve into an enchanted smile once more. "And shoes?" she inquired, enjoying the repartee. "Did you learn about women's tastes in shoes from six-year-old Melinda Briggs, too?"

He shook his head, an expression of distaste crossing his face. "Heavens no. In fact, as I recall Melin sported some nauseatingly cotton-candy pink tennies with little lavender bears printed on them. Awful things those," he grimaced in a way that made Sam laugh. "No, my knowledge of women's taste in shoes came from my dear old pops," he said with notable fondness.

Nonchalantly, he tightened the sash of his trench coat as he spoke. Sam noticed how the coat outlined his frame, accentuating his broad shoulders, narrowing to his waist and hips. "Pops owns a shop quite like this one back east. In Boston," he specified. "Seems that's how he and your uncle first met. At a trade convention many, many years ago."

"You're in the same business then?" she asked curiously, wondering if that was the reason for his visit to her uncle.

"Oh, no, not at all." He raised his hands emphatically. "Fortunately by the grace of God and all the angels in the heavens . . . the seraphims, I'm thinking, and those adorable chubby ones, what are they?"

"Cherubims?" She couldn't seem to control the smiles that kept tugging at her lips.

"Yes, thank you, cherubims." He nodded in gratitude, then paused in his explanation to study her face. "You have a poetic smile. Do you know that?" he asked as if in a trance.

Embarrassed by his scrutiny, heat rose to her cheeks once more. "I have no clue what you're talking about." She shook her head, shifting her eyes bashfully toward the floor.

Even he seemed bewildered by the words he'd blurted out. "Well, I—" his speech stumbled, "I'm not sure I do either." His feet shifted uneasily. "I suppose I mean your smile . . . it lights up your face . . . makes your eyes dance . . . warms onlookers' hearts. That's a bit poetic, don't you think?"

When she didn't respond, he bent slightly, tilting his head trying to get her to look his way. "I'm sorry if I embarrassed you," he offered in a hushed tone. "I didn't mean to at all. Perhaps I should stick to your original question?"

She glanced up at him and nodded, giving him a slight smile to let him know he was edging his way back into her good graces again.

He took a deep breath before continuing. "No, thankfully, I'm not at all inclined toward retail or financial consulting. Not like my three other brothers. Actually, as you may have guessed, I'm the rebel of the family." He paused and allowed her the alluring affect of his knee-weakening smile. A grin that made his full lips curl slightly at either end. And lit up his eyes impishly. "Which can be, uh, I'd say . . . really quite wonderful at times."

Ever staid and true, Sam never thought she'd be so easily drawn in and then held spellbound by something as silly as an accent. But it did have a hypnotic quality about it. Especially when dispensed by such an attractive Englishman.

Yet, there were other things she noticed instantly about Blake too. Appealing things like how genuine he seemed. How generous he was with his smiles . . . humor . . . compliments—even if they could be discomfiting at times. He also had an ease about him that made their conversation seem carefree and lighthearted, so unlike anything she and Prescott—

Prescott! A cloud of guilt fell heavy on her shoulders at the thought of him. The smile melted from her lips.

Oblivious, Blake pushed back his right cuff and glanced at the gold wristwatch on his wrist. "Ah, well. I'm going to be late for an appointment if I don't run. Though I admit, I hate to tear myself away from our enjoyable chat. Tell me," he said, tugging the cuff of his shirt and then his raincoat back into place, "are you involved in your uncle's business? Dom's buyer? Accountant? Shoe model?"

His slow, teasing smile followed the last two words, reviving her levity. "Actually, none of the above." She grinned.

"Hmm." He nodded thoughtfully. "Do you work nearby then?"

"Across the street," she answered a tad reluctantly. "For the county's Children's Services Agency."

His eyes lit up. "You work with children?"

"Well, in a way." She paused a moment, and before she could explain exactly what her job entailed, he was on to his next question.

"Do you have any?" he inquired, his voice sounding anxious.

Surely he's spied the engagement ring on my finger, she thought glancing down on her hands. *Well, maybe if I didn't have gloves on he might have* . . . she realized, chagrined.

Before going out into the brisk, rainy October day, she'd slipped on the pair of chartreuse gloves she kept in the top drawer of her desk. They'd been given to her last year as a Christmas present by a down-on-their-luck young couple she had helped to reunite with their baby boy.

Surely the gauche color and synthetic leather material of the gloves would have repulsed the Sterlings. But Sam loved them. Knowing whom they were from—and why they'd been given to her—brought a special warmth to her hands and heart.

"No, I don't," she answered, shaking her head.

It was the perfect opportunity to speak up and set the record straight. Tell him she wasn't married. At least not yet. Tell him all about the engagement. And about Prescott and their wedding coming up in three months. But then . . . did it really matter anyway? What were the chances she'd ever see the Englishman again?

"Do you?" she asked politely, glancing surreptitiously at his ring finger. It was bare as she assumed it would be. Certainly if he were married with children he'd be the type to tell the entire world about it. Always ready with a dozen photos or so in his wallet to show to anyone he came in contact with.

He shook his head. "But I miss my brothers' tykes. Saturday morning cartoons and the monkeys at the zoo are much more entertaining with a little bugger at your side, aren't they now?"

She laughed at his description. How easily she could picture him in a pair of plaid pajama bottoms in front of a television with a niece or nephew. His limbs sprawled out comfortably on a couch laughing at the antics of some cartoon character. Or even at the zoo making faces at the monkeys in their cages.

"Would you happen to have a business card with you?" he asked abruptly, much to her surprise. "Perhaps I can rent a child from your agency one day," he mused.

With a playful glint, his olive eyes teased her blue eyes. Unfortunately, they were mesmerizing as well.

"We're not actually in that business," she answered, her voice low. She knew his rental request was a ruse, and the thought made her heart pulse rapidly in her chest. Standing there, holding his gaze, it was openly apparent why he wanted her card.

And though it was tempting . . .

There was a matter of a fiancé to consider. Prescott. She couldn't in good conscious give Blake an easy means to contact her. It wouldn't be right. Besides, with the information they'd already shared—and with Uncle Dom not being one of Prescott's biggest fans—if Blake really wanted to locate her it wouldn't take much effort on his part.

"Sorry," she said, feeling badly for fibbing. "I'm fresh out."

"Well then . . ." He cocked his head and couldn't have looked more appealing as he said, "Perhaps I'll run into you again sometime?"

She started to say "no." No, it wasn't probable. Possible. Or a good idea in the least. But apparently Blake was, after all, like a son to her aunt and uncle. Besides that, the other women in the store were still keeping tabs on their semi-private conversation, all the while glancing at her enviously and scornfully. And at him, adoringly and protectively. These ladies might stone her to death if she wasn't kind to him. Actually, from the looks of them, they still might do that anyway. What did it hurt to be polite?

"I, um . . ." She nodded and shrugged her shoulders simultaneously. "Yes. Perhaps."

"Good then." He let his gaze linger just a moment longer. "Well, I'd best be off. It was wonderful meeting you," he said. Then he turned and walked toward Uncle Dominic who was finishing up with his return customer.

"Sir, always a pleasure," he addressed her uncle,

clasping him on the back again. They exchanged a few more words out of Sam's range of hearing.

It wasn't until Blake had turned up his collar to ward off the wet weather that he appeared to notice the store full of bewitched women staring after him.

"Ladies," he addressed them, tipping his head and smiling warmly. "A great afternoon to all you lovelies." The women returned his smile, and with that, he was on his way.

Chapter Two

"**S**omething else, isn't he?" Uncle Dom chuckled as he strolled over to Sam. Like everyone else in the shop, he was left beaming in Blake's wake. "He's had the same verve for life since he was yay high." Uncle Dom measured a yard of distance from the carpeted floor to his hand.

"He said you've known his family for a long time," Sam remarked casually, more interested than she wanted to let on—even to herself.

"For as long as I can remember," he said wistfully. He shrugged his shoulders which were beginning to show sloping signs of age. "You know, Samantha, your aunt and I never could have any children," he confessed quietly, rubbing his hands together. "Lord knows we wanted to more than anything. But even so, we feel we've been blessed to be a part of your life and a part of B.D.'s clan." He sighed contentedly.

Sam leaned over and gave him a peck on the cheek.

"You're too sweet, Uncle Dom. I'd say we're blessed to have you and Aunt Maria."

"Well, now . . ." Her uncle tucked his head modestly. "I just want you to know we think all of you have grown up to be very fine people," he said proudly as if the adults he'd known as children were his own sons and daughter.

"And amusing people, too," she retorted. "Blake certainly has a good sense of humor," she replied, wondering why she was still fishing for more information about the Englishman, though it did seem safe now that he was gone and it was doubtful they'd cross paths again.

Her uncle waved a hand at her as if she didn't know the half of it. "You wouldn't believe." He shook his head, looking somber once more. "Do you know when Phillip—the brother who's closest to B.D.'s age—was in the army reserves he was unexpectedly assigned to overseas duty. But Phillip was married by then and his wife was pregnant with their first child. And B.D., acting on his own volition—no prodding from anyone—volunteered to go in Phillip's place. He was stationed for over a year in Germany."

Sam's eyes widened in astonished admiration for the man she'd just met. "Seriously?"

Uncle Dominic nodded. "Phillip and Cara named the baby after him. Were happy to, of course." He paused as the words sunk in. "Yes, he's a humorous fellow, B.D. But there's much more to him than all of his jocular banter. Do you know he also finished in the top ten percent of his law class at Columbia?"

So he's a lawyer? Of course, she didn't know that either. And probably would have never guessed it. From what little she'd learned from her conversation with Blake, it was apparent he had an engaging personality. But obviously, he was more multi-faceted than that, much more intriguing.

"Why is he here?" she wondered out loud. "In Somersby, Ohio?"

"He said he had a few minutes to spare before his appointment with a realtor," her uncle explained. "Apparently, he's opening a law practice somewhere in town. Although," her uncle's forehead creased in bafflement, "I'm not sure why he'd leave his partnership in a prestigious firm in Boston to come here. That does seem odd, doesn't it?"

Sam's breath caught instantly. This B.D. person was moving to Somersby?

Hopefully if he did settle here, he'd find a quaint office on the outskirts of town and not right here in the Square—Somersby Square—which was actually a rectangle of restored historical buildings housing offices and shops all looking out onto a grassy park area in the center.

She couldn't imagine running into Blake Dawson in the morning on her way to the agency. Or bumping into him on her lunch hour as she had today. Or saying goodnight as they crossed paths on their way home in the evening.

"Speaking of odd, what were you thinking, eyeing those awful white pumps?" Her uncle asked in a low, discreet voice, evidently sharing Blake's opinion of the shoe . . . and actually her own as well.

She winced, totally dismayed, attempting to push unsettling thoughts of Blake aside and move onto her next problem. How to plan a wedding that would please everyone—most notably, Genevieve Elizabeth Sterling.

"I'm sorry to be so blunt, dear," her uncle apologized, "but I'm saying that kindly. That shoe is so . . . so . . . pedestrian. I carry it only for the meekest of women. And that's not at all how I think of you." He raised his eyebrows imploringly, looking to be forgiven.

"Well, thank you, I think . . ." She sighed, something she seemed to be doing a lot of lately—even well before her encounter with the Englishman. Although the thought of him did make her want to sigh too.

She felt so indecisive these days. Out of control. So unlike herself. Feeling the need to be nurtured instead of nurturing others. It felt comforting when Uncle Dom put his arm around her shoulders.

"Come now." He led her to the front of the store. "I've got just the thing to set your world straight again. Cookies!" he exclaimed, his eyes brightening. He held out a colorful platter to her. Slices of a Picasso design stared back at her from where cookies had once been.

"Take two; they're small," he advised. "And so are you. You're wilting away to nothing."

"Hardly," she countered. While the confections from her aunt's kitchen weren't the salve for all of life's problems, they did offer a delightful momentary reprieve from the daily struggle. Especially since Sam was a certified cookie addict. She took off her gloves and happily complied.

"Mmm . . ." she murmured, savoring the sweet combination of ingredients. Brownie-like chocolate. Macadamia nuts. Peanut butter morsels. Orange M & M's. Her taste buds exploded with joy. "These are incredible."

He smiled at her delighted response. "They're a special Halloween cookie your aunt calls 'Love at First Bite.' "

"I can certainly see why." She bit into the second cookie even more eagerly than the first. Uncle Dom watched over her, pleased. She knew he'd relay her pleasure to her aunt.

"Now tell me," he urged once the sugary cookies had sweetened her mood again. "What's troubling you?"

"Oh, Uncle Dom . . . don't worry about me," she said, absently brushing the crumbs from her hands and lips. "It's just the wedding . . ." her voice trailed off.

"The wedding?" His voice perked up.

Was that a glint of a smile shining in his eyes?

Uncle Dom ducked his head close to hers, speaking in a low conspiratorial whisper, "Having second thoughts, huh?"

Second thoughts? Wasn't that when you weren't sure if you'd said "yes" to the right person? And she was sure about that.

Wasn't she?

Prescott was a good guy, after all.

Right?

Movie star looks may not run in the Sterling genes, but Prescott could sure wear khaki pants, a blue blazer and loafers quite well. And he had a calm demeanor, rarely ever raised his voice. In fact, they'd never had a disagreement—ever! That was a plus, wasn't it?

Of course, it *was* slightly difficult to argue with a person you rarely saw. Prescott was tied up quite often, regularly escorting his mother to some sort of social function or another. Many social functions, in fact. And dinners and meetings and . . .

Sam felt a twinge of annoyance gnaw at her and

caught herself. She needed to squelch these feelings, these kinds of thoughts, before the wedding. Instead she should be pleased the man she was going to marry was so very kind and attentive to his widowed mother. And she should be proud of his place within the Sterling clan.

While Sam was a champion for the city's needy children, he was a champion of the arts and his family made many improvements in the community. Lucrative improvements, true, but still . . . together, as a couple, she'd always thought they could better the world—or at least Somersby County.

And that he had to spend so much time with his mother sorting out the incredible load of family affairs—that just made sense, didn't it? And really, wasn't it a good thing? After all, she had her own time-consuming job at the agency.

Thankfully, Prescott never pressured her about her responsibilities at work—though Genevieve always had some subtle comment to make. Either about Sam's "silly" visits to the inner city schools. Or about how Sam should consider leaving the agency once she and Prescott were married and Sam became "one of them."

But unlike his mother, Prescott never really made many comments about Sam's job.

Thank goodness for that! I'm way too busy to have a man wanting to spend every minute with me—to be breathing down my neck!

And Prescott certainly wasn't doing that. He wasn't breathing down her neck . . . or whispering sweet things in her ear. He didn't even like to cuddle or hold hands much.

But then, he was a by-product of his reserved upbringing. The flip side of that was he never ever pressured her about being intimate before marriage. In fact, it seemed he did well in restraining himself in that department. In the six months they'd been engaged, they'd never shared more than goodnight kisses. Perfunctory kisses. Brotherly. Vanilla.

Probably not the same sort of kisses the Englishman delivered . . . Her body shivered involuntarily.

"I don't know, Uncle Dom." Flustered by her imaginings and feeling guiltier than ever, she ran her fingers through her hair, caught a strand and began to twist it anxiously. "I'm not sure what kind of thoughts I'm having exactly. I'm usually good at making decisions, but with this wedding—I don't know—I can't seem to make any."

She raised her arms in a hopeless gesture. "Every florist I visit, every catering menu I read, I feel like Genevieve is looking over my shoulder. And then Prescott doesn't have time to help . . .'

"I just don't know how to make everyone happy." Frustrated, her hands fell limp against her thighs. She rolled her eyes, loathing the sound of her own whiny voice.

Uncle Dom drummed his fingers methodically on the desk, each nail making a perfect click. At first he seemed reluctant to speak, but as the fire in his cheeks increased, it appeared he couldn't hold back his burning desire to do so. The steady rhythm of his nails stopped as he confided in her.

"I could literally kick myself for ever introducing you to that awful woman. Somehow I thought the introduction might benefit your fundraising efforts at the agency. But that hasn't happened," he muttered, tightly clenching his teeth.

"But Uncle Dom," she placed a comforting hand on his arm, "if you hadn't introduced me to Genevieve, I may have never met Prescott."

"Yes, well, then there's that . . ." Uncle Dom's voice drifted. She noticed his lips contorted into a wary expression before saying more. "Trust me, Samantha, I've had many dealings with Genevieve."

His dark eyes grew darker as he spoke of Chausseures' landlord. Unfortunately, the shop was housed in one of the many Somersby Square buildings that the Sterling family owned. "Your future mother-in-law is overbearing and there's no way on earth to ever please her. And as for Prescott. Well, Prescott is so . . . he's so . . ."

"Amiable? Amicable?" She completed his sentence. The words were meant to be complimentary. But, why didn't they sound that way? Why did they sound so lackluster . . . so much like *mealy-mouthed* or *wishy-washy?*

"Whatever." Uncle Dom raised an eyebrow. "Honestly, dear, I probably shouldn't say this," he leaned toward her, his tone gentle, "but I don't know if Prescott will ever stand up to his mother." He sighed disconsolately before continuing. "So I suppose what I'm saying in all of this is—do what makes you happy. With that pair," he shrugged as if the matter was beyond reasoning, "what else can you do?"

Sam studied her uncle's face for a moment, pondering all he had said. It was more true than she wanted to admit. Genevieve always wanted control. And Prescott, for whatever reason, was always more than willing to let her have it. In reality, he was more than just kind and attentive to his mother. He was at her every beck and call.

But maybe it was because Sam hadn't really asserted

herself with the pair of them. She simply needed to let her fiancé and his mother know she had opinions and desires of her own. Surely they would understand.

"You're right, Uncle Dom." She hugged him feeling somewhat relieved, a new-found determination surging inside of her. "I'm going to plot everything out on paper. All the things that *I* want for the wedding. Then I'll list all the pros and cons, and go from there."

"You're still making out pro and con lists?" He chuckled, apparently amused that she still followed the decision-making process she'd employed since college.

"How else does everyone make decisions?" she asked sincerely.

Uncle Dom looked at her with a loving smile. "I don't know about everyone else, Samantha. But I do know about you. You have a good mind and a caring heart." He took her hand and gave it a pat. "Use them both. You'll figure out what's right."

Despite the persistent, plopping raindrops, Sam's footsteps felt light as she made her way across the lawn of the Square back to the agency.

Uncle Dom's advice couldn't have been better.

It was time she took charge. Took the reins back on her personal life—most especially the matter of the wedding—just like she did in her professional life. After all, at the agency she made difficult decisions every day. Decisions that changed people's lives, for goodness' sake. Surely, she was capable of picking out bridesmaids' heels, a reception menu and floral arrangements without Genevieve Sterling's approval.

With renewed energy, she entered Somersby's Children's Services Agency, her home away from home.

Most of the other social workers had offices on the second and third floors of the renovated brownstone. But her office was on the first floor along with a conference room and a small reception area.

Though a somber, rainy day atmosphere hovered inside, April, the agency's receptionist, sat wide-eyed and intent, reading a *True Romance* magazine at the reception desk.

"Did you get some lunch?" Sam pushed back the hood of her coat, and undid the rain slick buttons.

April nodded, folding the magazine in half, concealing the cover, attempting to discreetly slip it into her desk drawer. Using both hands at once, she simultaneously tucked her long, straight, coal-colored hair behind her ears, both of which were adorned with one small and one large hoop earring.

"Ryan made organic chili for me." She smoothed the skirt of her empire waist hippie dress, colored in swirls of autumn gold and burnt orange.

Sam tried to picture April's burly husband with his lineman build bent over the stove making an "organic" anything for his new bride. "Wow, I'm impressed. I didn't know he could cook."

"Uh, he can't," April cringed, though a fond smile lit her face. "Since he knows I'm into health foods, he's working on preparing some organic meals for us."

Sam chuckled. "Not too successful, huh?"

April shook her head, earrings swaying. "I'm about ready to chuck my healthy ideals for a greasy burger, fries and a shake," she replied, handing Sam a bulky legal-sized envelope that had been delivered while she was out along with a solitary phone message. "Anything to let my taste buds know they're still alive!"

Sam grinned, and started to head toward her office.

"Oh, about the phone message," April called after her. "It's from Mr. Sterling." Sam turned to see her fidgeting with the tan leather choker adorning her neck. "He called to remind you about the Aronoff Center fundraiser tonight. Said his mother will be 'most disappointed' if you can't come," she quoted properly.

His mother would be disappointed?

"Thanks, April," Sam replied evenly, trying to hide her annoyance. Then she turned on her heels and stomped into her office. Tossing her damp coat and purse onto one of the extra cushioned chairs, she huffed over to her desk.

Mother, mother, mother—oh, brother!

What Genevieve wants. What Genevieve demands. What Genevieve expects, she fumed to herself, dropping into her swivel chair.

And what about Prescott? Would he miss her? Would he be disappointed if his fiancée weren't there? You'd think any red-blooded male would be—but then again it *was* Prescott . . .

She slammed the oversized legal envelope on the desk a little harder than she intended to. It landed with a loud thud.

It really was all about Genevieve, wasn't it? she realized more starkly than ever.

Her office door opened suddenly, jarring her thoughts. April poked her head in. "Uh," she said, fidgeting with her necklace again, "everything okay in here?" she asked, referring to the loud noise.

"Just perfect." Sam's lips tightened.

"Well, um, Brittany Walters is on line one for you."

April sounded hesitant. "I can take a message if you want."

"No, I'll take it," Sam said. At the mention of her former intern's name, Sam's mood brightened somewhat. Brittany had been a great help at the agency two summers ago before starting at Thomas Bentley College several hours away in West Virginia. Beyond that, Sam had simply liked the girl. She'd felt like an older sister, enjoying their chats together even though over the past year their talks had grown fewer and farther between.

"Hey, Brittany." Sam sat back in her chair, trying to relax. "How is everything?"

"Okay," the girl answered somewhat meekly.

"I haven't heard from you in a while," she ribbed her. "And you're already into your sophomore year. That's hard to believe."

"I know," Brittany replied. "Sorry I haven't called or e-mailed."

"No problem. I'm sure you're busy. It's good to hear from you no matter when it is," Sam said sincerely. Brittany definitely didn't sound like her typical bubbly self, Sam observed. "Britt, is everything okay?"

"Sure," Brittany's voice brightened—a bit too much. "I just wanted to say 'hi.' I'm in town visiting a friend."

"Oh, yeah? Do you have time to stop by?"

"Um, not really. I'm leaving first thing in the morning. Super early," Brittany said, leaving no room for a breakfast get-together. "Um," she paused. "I heard you're engaged."

"You heard right," Sam quipped.

"Wow, and to a Sterling. That's pretty awesome."

Sam was sure her situation sounded like a fairy tale, a dream come true to a young girl like Brittany. The millionaire fiancé. The white picket fence that went on for acres, swimming pool, and lawn care service.

But there was also the nightmarish mother-in-law. If Brittany only knew! Sam winced inwardly. "How about you? Are you and Justin still dating?"

"We're—well, it's a long story. And—" she stammered. "I've got to go. My friend needs the phone, okay?" There was a momentary silence between them.

"Hey, well, call again soon," Sam ventured. "Before you're a junior, all right?"

Brittany chuckled slightly. "Sure. I will."

After hanging up the phone, Sam sat still for a moment thinking about Brittany. Something didn't sound quite right with her. She had certainly sounded as vulnerable as her nineteen years.

Hopefully she knows she can call if she really needs help with anything, Sam thought as she started organizing the papers on her desk. Among them Prescott's phone message which made her groan out loud.

She really wasn't in the mood for Genevieve tonight, and she should stay and work on the case files overflowing her in basket anyway. Right? Wasn't her work more important than feeding Genevieve Sterling's insatiable ego after all?

Decisively, she called Prescott's cell phone to tell him of her change in plans before she could change her mind. Thankfully, his voice mail picked up. Who needed to hear the lack of longing in his voice? Or listen once again about how disappointed *Genevieve* would be by her absence. Especially when, in fact, that wasn't even totally true. Genevieve wouldn't miss her presence. She'd simply be irritated that Sam hadn't followed her wishes.

How did I get myself into this situation? she wondered, her stomach feeling sick and hollow.

But in reality she knew.

Rummaging through her desk drawers, her fingers sifted through pamphlets, contracts, schedules, and agency memos. "It's in here somewhere," she mumbled to herself wondering at the term 'paperless society.'

Finally, the sheet she was looking for. She smoothed it out on the desk before her, studying the neat column of words penned in her own precise handwriting.

PRESCOTT STERLING

PROS   CONS
Decent looking, good height
Kind and diplomatic—esp.
with his widowed mother
Nice smile, good orthodontia work
Financially sound
Wants to wait to be intimate till
wedding night

*Children

That's how she'd gotten into it.

True to her nature, right after Prescott proposed to her, she'd done a P&C list before she'd given him her answer. Whereas most fortune-seeking females would've said "yes" merely because of the Sterling family name, that really wasn't a deciding factor for her. Instead, she had to plot out Prescott's qualities. And on paper, it all looked good. Logical. No "cons" at all.

But now, looking at the crisp black words on the stark white paper, she realized "cons" weren't the only thing missing. Something else was lacking as well. There was no passion, no surge of emotion to be read in between the lines written there.

Even with the issue of children, she'd been passive— passionless—she recalled as her eyes focused on the word on the page.

At the time of Prescott's proposal, kids had been an iffy issue between them so she'd simply noted it with an asterisk. But even that hadn't stopped her from saying "yes" to him.

True, at one point in her life she'd imagined herself as a mother to an entire house full of rambunctious kids. But then with her parents' separation, she had grown less enthused about the notion. Her ideas about the "perfect family life" were completely shattered. So when Prescott didn't seem very willing to commit to the idea of children, she had dropped the issue. She hadn't pushed it.

Lacing a pencil through her fingers, she plopped back in her chair with a weary sigh.

You have a good mind . . . a caring heart. Her uncle's words echoed in her mind. *Use them both.*

Obviously that advice had come six months too late! Though, honestly, would she have heeded Uncle Dom's suggestion all those months ago?

Doubtful.

Her heart had still been so full of disappointment over her parents' break up even then. Isn't that why she'd been so clinical about Prescott's proposal? Why she'd chosen logic over passion?

But with the passing of time came the easing of bitterness. Who knew how long it would take before she completely accepted her parents' decision? At least she could tell her heart was healing. She could feel herself opening up again and that was a good thing.

Like today. With Blake.

True, even six months ago she wouldn't have been downright rude to the Englishman. Especially once she realized how fond her uncle was of him. She would've talked to Blake and might have even enjoyed their conversation somewhat. But today . . . it had been more than enjoyable.

Her heart had felt light. Accepting. Her smile—*poetic*. That's how he described it, and it felt that way as she stood talking to him. Surely, it must mean that she was healing. *And that, yes, like most other females I'm a sucker for an English accent*, she grinned wanly to herself. Certainly it couldn't be anything more than that. Especially not with someone she'd just met.

And now that she was becoming whole again, she should put all of that renewed energy into her and Prescott's relationship. Surely two people who could be so zealous about their causes could develop a passionate relationship with one another. *Maybe I'll even turn him into a cuddler,* she mused to herself.

And I'll even try hard with his mother, she vowed, sitting up straighter in the chair, making notes to herself. No, she wouldn't let Genevieve run over her, of course. But she'd find a way to maintain her patience with the haughty woman and her demands.

She'd have to be diplomatic though; she stirred uneasily in her chair. Bucking Genevieve too brazenly was like poking a stick at an angry rattler. Genevieve could rear up and retaliate in any number of ways.

Like harm Uncle Dom's business . . . the sickening thought crossed her mind as she pictured her uncle's shop and the building owned by the Sterling matriarch. Yes, she had to be just as tactful with Genevieve as she'd learned to be with the families she dealt with through the agency.

But . . . enough about me. Sam shook her head, trying to shove thoughts of her personal affairs aside. It was time to get back to work. There were other people besides her searching for happiness. Couples who had already vowed their love to one another. Couples willing to extend that love to babies in need of a caring home environment.

She grabbed for the hefty legal envelope on her desk, figuring it contained documents pertaining to the McCafferty adoption. How cute the two of them had been, she recalled. Erin and Will McCafferty.

Mid-thirty professionals, both so successful yet both ready to sacrifice prestigious positions and lucrative incomes to take turns staying at home with a little one. At their first appointment in Sam's office, they sat holding hands the entire time, hanging anxiously onto every word she said. And onto each other.

Hopefully, she'd be giving them good news soon, she thought, tearing at the end of the envelope, pulling out the legal documents.

Strange. It wasn't the McCafferty papers at all. It was—?

She glanced at the letterhead, but didn't recognize the name of the law firm. Then she went on to read the first paragraph of the cover letter. That was all she needed to see.

Staring at the words, her blood ran cold. Her heartbeat drummed in her ears. She gasped for breath.

Chapter Three

"**O**h, my God!" Blake heard Sam exclaim, so absorbed in whatever she was reading she didn't even realize he was standing there in her office doorway.

At first he thought he should reconsider. Maybe tiptoe back out of her office, even though the retro-attired young lady at the front desk had just waved him on ahead.

It hadn't taken much to convince the free-spirited receptionist he was harmless, a friend of the family. Especially when she was so tied up in a rather romantic-sounding phone call with—well, hopefully with her husband, he thought, catching tidbits of the conversation.

Still . . . maybe he shouldn't have even come. Especially now, he found himself thinking, seeing Sam's head bowed disconsolately over some papers. But then—

Could he really have stopped himself? It's not every day he met a female and went blubbering on and on about angels. Seraphims. Cherubims. How ridiculous he must've sounded!

But he hadn't been able to get the idea of angels off his mind. Because that's how she had looked to him. Blonde, shiny shoulder-length hair crowning her head like a halo. Eyes as bright and blue as the sky itself. And a face—creamy complexion and all—that was utterly heavenly.

Yes, an overall angelic look. That's how she'd appeared to him. Except for those chartreuse gloves, of course. A smile tugged at his lips at the memory of them. The gloves weren't especially divine. Even so, there was something curiously endearing about them.

And now here she was pouring over some document, looking so distraught it made him wince.

"I take it my timing is somewhat horrid," he said, his voice low and apologetic.

Sam looked up at the sound, her heavenly face distorted in dismay. An angel in distress, to be sure. In fact, she looked even more perplexed than she had a moment before—and understandably so. She must've been startled to see him standing there.

But then her features relaxed somewhat, and she attempted a fragment of a smile. "No, I'm just surprised," she said, shaking her head slightly.

He wasn't sure if she was referring to his impromptu visit or the paper in front of her.

"Everything all right?" He approached her desk and noticed the familiar look of a legal document in her hand, saw the clouds of concern in her celestial blue eyes. "Ah. Legal matters." He crinkled his nose in distaste. "Yes. Those can be impossibly upsetting at times. But I do happen to know an excellent lawyer . . ." He raised his eyebrows in a sympathetic slant, and tried out his most compassionate, charming smile on her.

She declined his help and the smile with a shake of her head. "I couldn't . . . really."

"Surely you can . . . really." He nodded at her encouragingly. "After all, we *are* going to be neighbors. That's what I ran over to tell you." His eyes perused her face, trying to read her expression. "I'm taking the space right above Gabby's Galleria. Owned by some Sterling Enterprises, I learned." As he recalled the meeting, he added, "Not the most pleasant people I've ever signed a contract with, let me tell you."

She sat with her mouth open—a lovely mouth, he thought—but still, a little disconcerting. Was she happy or pained by his news? he wondered. It was hard to tell and it was moments before she spoke.

"I—what?" she stammered which really didn't give him much of a clue.

"I apologize," he said, noting her confusion. "I burst in unannounced with some silly news. You're obviously in the middle of something direly important here. So, please, let me redeem myself by offering my legal services once again." He swept his arm in a knightly fashion in front of him.

"Seriously, I couldn't," she tried to dissuade him once more.

"Playing hard to get, huh?" he asked, trying to cajole her, lighten her mood. "I love that in a client," he said, lifting the document from her desk.

He usually wasn't so forward. Didn't really mean to be pushy. But it was obvious she was in awful straits, and he'd do anything to help her. It was pure nonsense that she refused his aid.

However, one glimpse at the legalese with practiced eyes, and it was his turn to stutter. "I—um," was all he could manage for a moment, too startled to know exactly what to say after reading the cover letter.

The cover letter which outlined a pre-nuptial agreement.

A pre-nuptial agreement between one Samantha Stevenson and one Prescott Sterling d/b/a Sterling Enterprises, Inc.

"I agree," he said, shaking his head solemnly, placing the contract back on her desk blotter. "That *is* a rather disturbing document."

He shrank back, sinking into the bluish-green cushioned chair in front of her desk. He felt something goose him as he settled into the seat. Her leather purse and damp coat. Unthinkingly, he moved them both to the empty chair beside him.

"I'm sure you tried to tell me a million times." He gestured to her with understanding arms, the fabric of his trench coat rustling in the silence of the room. "Obviously I didn't hear."

"Actually that's not true," she admitted in a soft voice. "I didn't try." She turned her head, looking away from him. She seemed to be embarrassed.

Embarrassed for him and his apparent interest in her? Or embarrassed because she had felt something between them, too? Something unique and special, just as he had felt, as they stood there talking together an hour or so ago?

Don't be ridiculous! he reminded himself. The woman is engaged to be married. And obviously to an extremely wealthy man if the voluminous size of the pre-nup meant anything—which it usually did.

Why would she divulge her love interests to him? It

wasn't as if she owed him anything. They were merely strangers. Acquaintances who had shared nothing more than a conversation. Even if it had felt like something more than that to him.

Concealing his disappointment, he clapped his hands together, and righted himself in the chair. "Well, no matter," he assured her, brushing the disappointment and embarrassment aside. After all, this wasn't about him at the moment, he remembered, noting the lines of concern contorting her lovely face.

"Positively shell-shocked, aren't you?" Sympathy crept into his voice.

He saw her jaw tighten. "You could say that."

"You didn't expect a pre-nup? Even given the vast wealth I'm assuming your fiancé possesses?" It seemed a naïve notion, he thought. Not totally implausible, but naïve—at least from a lawyer's point of view.

"My fiancé," she said dryly, "and his mother."

"Oh." *Mother-in-law problems already*, he assumed, noting her tone.

She drew herself up in the chair, shaking her head haughtily, a gesture that seemed totally unlike her. He watched as the tossed blonde hair settled into place around her face, and sensed she was working hard to stay under control. Trying to let defiance mask her hurt.

She crossed her arms over the bodice of her olive knit dress before she spoke. "I don't even know what all the Sterlings own. It's not something Prescott and I have ever discussed much. And it's never mattered because I have never, ever cared about the Sterling money. Their businesses. Their properties. Their fortune," she said the words with disgust. "Besides, is that what my fiancé thinks of me? Does he think I'm some money-seeking person? Is that who he thinks I am?" Her voice rose, sounding crushed and indignant that anyone would think of her that way.

"Many women *would* care, Sam," his voice soft in comparison to hers.

She stared him in the eye, her glare unwavering with honesty. "I'm not most women."

No, she wasn't, he realized. It seemed she really didn't care about the money, the social status. And most likely the Sterlings had realized that too. Probably a rare find for a man of Prescott's means.

"Hard as it is, Sam, you can't take this personally," he told her. "A pre-nup is not necessarily drawn up as a comment on your character. It just makes for smart business," he said, sounding completely practical. Though, if the truth were known and their positions switched, he'd be feeling exactly the same way she did.

"Well, to me," she said brusquely without looking up at him, "signing a pre-nup is like saying you don't expect the marriage to last to begin with. And anyway, marriage isn't supposed to be about money and business." She shuffled around the papers on her desk, pretending to be totally composed. It almost worked until she spoke again. "It's supposed to be about lo—"

Suddenly her composure dissolved, her voice quivered, the word never quite making it out of her mouth.

And as much as he hated to leave, he knew it was the time to go. Time to let the woman salvage what was left of her dignity. But as he got up from the chair, he stood there for a moment, torn.

There was nothing he wanted to do more than to walk

around the side of her desk, wrap his arms around her, and comfort her.

He took a bold step forward. But then he stopped . . . and thought better of it. If he took her in his arms now, it might make things a bit easier for her. But after touching her, knowing the feel of her, things might be much more difficult for him. Would he want to let her go?

Instead he pointed to the pre-nuptial papers laying on her desktop. "Bring the agreement to my office in the morning. Right above the Galleria." He worked at forming a slight smile. "Truly, you'd be doing me a great favor. My first client, you know? After that, the rest, as they say, is a piece of cake."

A carefree front. A light-hearted façade. Not at all what he was feeling as he reluctantly left her in the quiet of her office.

Will I see her again? He wondered somberly, treading down the cement steps of the agency, back out into the dreary, drizzly day. *Tomorrow? Or anytime soon?*

Sam poured the steamy chamomile tea into a thermal cup, snapped on the lid, then bustled around her house gathering up the rest of her things for work. Her car keys from the hook in the kitchen. A paperback novel she said she'd bring in for April. Her purse. Briefcase.

And, oh yes. As much as she wanted to, she couldn't forget the prenuptial agreement. She'd need it for her appointment with Blake first thing this morning.

She deposited all her belongings on an antique church pew in her foyer, everything except for her leather briefcase. Instead she carried it into her bedroom, and picked up the burdensome agreement from her oak nightstand. Barely touching it with her fingertips as if it were tingled with poison, she slipped it into her satchel. That small task accomplished, she stood still for a moment and let out a weary sigh.

Stunned. That's how she felt. Still completely stunned. And now tired, too, after a long, restless night. Before going to sleep, she had tried to read over sections of the document, wanting to see if she could make some sense of it. But it didn't make for relaxing bedtime reading.

Besides, she realized, the contents of the document didn't even matter to her. It was the idea of the pre-nup itself that was most disturbing. So she had tossed it back on her nightstand then turned out her bedside lamp. But she couldn't manage to turn off her mind quite as easily, wrestling with questions most of the night.

A tumble of questions that still plagued her this morning . . .

Was the agreement something Genevieve had demanded Prescott do? Or had he acted all on his own? Did he really think it was necessary—didn't he know her any better than that? Why hadn't he forewarned her? How could he be so callous?

And most upsetting of all—

Was this really the kind of family she wanted for herself?

A sickly taste rose in the back of her throat, and she managed to swallow it back. The last question was the only one she could answer for herself. But she couldn't make herself do it. Couldn't face it.

Not just yet at least. For now, she'd leave it unanswered. Wait until she met with Blake. Maybe he had some kind of lawyer logic that she could buy. Something to say that would make this situation palatable. Salvageable.

With leather satchel in hand, she walked back into the foyer now saturated with streaks of sunshine. Light poured in through the palladium window above her front door, and she caught a glimpse of herself in the rectangular mirror above the pew. Gray sweater. Long gray flannel skirt. Sad grays in contrast to the glimmers of sunlight that danced around her face, set her hair all aglow.

What would Blake Dawson have to say right this moment? she wondered. Probably something cheery. Something like, "It's a brand new day, Sam. Everything looks better in the morning, doesn't it?"

Without even realizing it, her reflection smiled back. A fond smile, playing on her lips at the thought of him. What an upbeat guy he was! His light-hearted spirit contagious, she mused as she passed up her dark, black leather jacket, opting for the bright-colored cranberry fleece one instead.

Donning her crimson coat, she felt a little better as she gathered up her things and stepped outside. Outside, into the new day, bright with golden sunshine and blue, blue skies.

And yet . . . all she saw was pink. And more pink.

Sitting on her front porch, alongside a pink diaper bag dotted with friendly white elephants, Sam saw a soft, pink canopy. The fuzzy blanket covered a gray infant-carrier with a checkered pink cushion.

Sam stood still almost afraid to move. She looked to the left at her neighbor's yard; to the right, where a retired couple lived. Then she scanned the quiet, tree-lined cul-de-sac. But there was nothing. No car. No movement. No one to be seen.

Taking a deep breath, she knelt down, and cautiously, curiously lifted a corner of the blanket.

She peaked underneath to see . . . more pink. A pink and yellow knit hat. With a matching fuzzy, woolly, pink and yellow one-piece zip-up. All on a precious baby girl. With teensy carnation-pink hands fidgeting. Rosy cheeks glowing. And blue eyes staring. At Sam. Leaving her breathless. Melting her heart.

Chapter Four

"**I** see you've brought along a chaperone," Blake greeted Sam as she stood outside his office door, gripping the infant seat with both hands like an over-sized picnic basket.

"Honestly," he shifted his gaze from Sam to the baby girl buckled inside the carrier and whispered, "I'm not the rogue she thinks I am," he pleaded in mock defense.

The baby girl cooed up at him, the sound so sweet, it made Sam smile. *That British accent works wonders on females of all ages*, she mused.

"Come in, ladies." He ushered Sam into his office with a motion of his hand. His nearly bare office, she noticed, had only a pair of lone wooden chairs sitting in the middle of the room and a highboy table placed squarely between them. His navy suit coat hung from the back of one of the chairs.

"Charming decor," she said with a teasing giggle, nodding at the austere setup. She was surprised at the gaiety in her voice. Surprised she was even in the mood to make a witty comment. Especially after the shock of the pre-nup yesterday. The lack of sleep last night. And the hurt she'd been feeling just hours before whenever she thought of Prescott.

But suddenly she felt nearly giddy. It was crazy, she knew. She should've been positively stressed to have a baby girl dropped on her doorstep. Dropped into her life. But instead she had lifted the little one out of the infant seat, touched the baby's warm cheek to her own, and then she'd felt it. A natural attachment—a love so complete and sure—unlike anything she'd ever experienced before.

Were her feelings intensified because of her present problems with Prescott? she wondered. Or were they just as real as they felt? She wasn't sure. All she knew is that suddenly her uncertainties about motherhood simply faded away. She felt reborn. Alive. Buoyant. At one with the sunshine.

"I know, I know," Blake was saying, straightening his striped tie back into place, running his fingers through his thick crop of hair. "When I suggested you stop by this morning, I completely forgot I didn't have a stick of office furniture. But a trip to the store, and I'll be up to my nose in desks and bookcases. That's easy enough to take care of."

"Here," he said approaching her and the baby, "let me hold this beautiful creature while you take off your jacket."

He reached out his arms, and instantly she felt reluctant to give up custody of her newly acquired gift—even for a moment. A surge of protectiveness came over her, tightening her grip on the carrier's handles.

But it's Blake, she reminded herself. Practically a godson to Uncle Dom. A comfort to clumsy Melinda Briggs. A godsend to his brother Phillip. And though she barely knew him, a person who seemed most willing to help her in any situation.

With a nod, she relinquished the baby girl to him. Already transformed to a doting mother hen, she watched him carry the infant seat over to the table, handling it carefully, adroitly—not like a sack of potatoes, but like the precious cargo it was.

He set the carrier on the tabletop, crooning to the infant girl all the while. "What a lovely you are," he declared sweetly. "Big blue eyes. Going to have all the blokes falling for those, aren't you? Little heartbreaker."

Folding her coat over her arms, hugging it to her body, Sam listened and watched. Yes, he definitely had a way with the ladies, she smiled, totally convinced.

With the crisp white sleeves of his dress shirt rolled up, his muscular arms appeared strong and capable. Yet his voice was gentle, his hands caring as he pushed back the blanket tucked around the infant, getting a better look at her.

"She's adorable," he told Sam, turning to look at her, keeping a steady hand on the carrier all the while.

"A client of yours?" he asked.

"Not exactly." At least she assumed it wasn't. How would she know? There hadn't been a note.

"Godchild? Niece?"

"No and no. I'm an only child."

"Oh." He shrugged, turning back to the baby. "What's her name?

"I don't know."

The lack of answers didn't seem to phase him. He seemed satisfied to go on talking to the little one, sticking his index finger near her tiny hand, letting her wrap her entire fist around it.

Sam stepped closer, hugging her coat even tighter, not sure how to begin an explanation. Not that Blake seemed to require one.

"I found her. On my doorstep this morning."

She braced herself for his startled reaction, for his on-slaught of questions. *Had she contacted the police? What was she planning to do?* But he didn't seem to flinch, so she continued.

"I know I was meant to have her. I mean—there was a diaper bag. She was still warm. And the timing was perfect." She stood back, admiring Blake admire the baby. "It was intentional. I know it was. Someone who knows . . . knows my schedule."

"Someone who knows Sam is a nice lady who'll take good care of you, little one," he whispered assuredly to the baby.

For one lucid moment on her way here, she'd won-dered why she'd pointed the car toward Blake's office. Blake whom she'd only met yesterday.

She told herself it was because she had an appointment with him, and since he didn't have a phone there was no way to cancel it. An important appointment to go over a pre-nup—the pre-nup which she hadn't even loaded into her car.

But now, watching him interact with the baby girl . . . Sam knew exactly why she'd come to Blake first. Be-cause in her heart she knew he wouldn't judge her. Wouldn't hustle her off to the police station. Wouldn't admonish her. Or preach to her.

She shivered, the thought of keeping—having—a baby girl in her life exciting her beyond belief. How she had ever fooled herself into thinking that helping children through her work was the same as raising a child of her own, she'd never know. And why she'd almost let her parents' differences—and Prescott's indifference toward parenting—almost rob her of a role so intrinsically right for her was just as perplexing.

But then . . . she had never had direct charge over a little baby's life. Never knew what it felt like to be so needed. One on one, up close and personal, for every detail of survival. Suddenly, her existence seemed full of a purpose and passion like she'd never known.

"It *is* a bit chilly in here, isn't it?" Blake said, noting her shiver. "I'm not sure they've regulated the heat yet." He paused, looking at his watch thoughtfully. "What time do you need to be at work?"

"I already called in," she confided to him. "I'm taking a day—or two—off," she said uncertainly.

"Well, ladies, what say we go for some breakfast? Eggs. Bacon. Formula?" He nodded to the baby girl. She gurgled at him in response.

Settling into the red vinyl booth at the out-of-the-way diner seemed as natural as anything for the three of them. Sam placed the carrier on the Formica-topped table, keeping careful watch that it didn't topple while she shrugged out of her jacket. At her side instantly, Blake helped her out of her coat, his hand brushing against her arms, sending an unexpected tingle up to her cheeks.

Standing there holding her coat in one hand, and the diaper bag in the other, she had to admit he certainly appeared comfortable in this new role.

And adorable, too, she thought a bit guiltily, as she watched him hang her coat on a hook outside the booth, and place the elephant-dotted diaper bag on the seat next to him.

Before sitting herself, Sam removed the baby's hat, revealing a few stray wisps of fine golden hair. Then she unzipped the pink one-piece covering, tugging gently at the baby's arms, releasing them from the confines of the outerwear. The baby seemed to appreciate it, her arms moving slightly with a newfound freedom. Sam wondered if she should remove the zip-up all the way, and decided she would.

Unbuckling the seat, she lifted the little girl into her arms where she seemed a natural, wonderful fit. Without even having to say a word, Blake reached up and removed the dangling outerwear the rest of the way.

Sam hated to let go of the baby girl, she felt so good in her arms. But she buckled her back into her seat anyway where she and Blake could both admire her.

Instantly, Blake put his hand up, testing the air over the baby's head. "Think it's a bit drafty," he announced. He pulled out the blanket stuffed into the sides of the carrier, then covered the baby's legs.

"Really?" Sam countered. "I'm feeling slightly warm." She moved the blanket slightly lower.

The repartee was friendly, their differences inconsequential. Neither had seen the baby without her hat and outerwear, and every time she moved or fidgeted they looked across the table at one another and smiled.

For a moment, Sam caught herself glancing around at the tables of early morning patrons wondering if she and Blake and the baby looked suspicious to anyone. If anyone could possibly tell the baby wasn't hers . . . and for that matter, neither was Blake.

But really how could they?

More likely they looked the epitome of a happy young family . . . a pair of mom and dad executives, having breakfast with their baby daughter before dropping her off at childcare for the day. That seemed confirmed when the waitress arrived at their table, carrying a pot of coffee.

"Need an eye opener?" she asked. They nodded, and she turned the cups over on their saucers and poured, then set the pot down on the table.

"Oh, isn't she a cutie?" She gave the baby a giant red-lipstick grin. "What's her name?" she asked, digging in her pockets for her pad and pencil.

Immediately, Sam's face flushed at the question. Her heart picked up pace. But Blake, as usual, came to the rescue.

"Princess," he piped up, saluting the waitress with his charming sideways smile.

Though past middle age, the woman warmed to him with a girlish giggle. "Princess? Aw, that's so sweet." She glanced at Sam enviously. "Proud daddy, huh?"

"The proudest," Sam affirmed, her eyes gleaming.

Once the waitress rushed off to put in their breakfast order, Sam leaned across the table. "Maybe we *should* give the baby a name," she half-whispered to Blake. "I mean in case someone asks again. Maybe something like . . . I don't know . . . Colleen."

"Colleen?" Blake appeared taken back, sitting upright in the booth. "That sounds rather Irish, don't you think?"

"Well, do you have any other suggestions?"

"I don't know. How about—how about—Theodosia?" He seemed to pluck the name out of the air.

Sam crinkled her nose. "Theodosia? Is that really a name? It sounds so frilly."

"Don't like frilly, do you? All right," he paused and thought some more. "How about Jane?"

"Too plain." She shook her head.

They sat silent for a moment, gazing at the baby in the carrier, sizing her up. Finally, Sam blurted out, "Emma! What do you think of Emma?"

A smile grazed Blake's lips. "Emma. Princess Emma. I like it. Do you like it, Emma?" He turned to the baby girl. She cooed at the sound of his voice. "She likes it."

They chuckled at Emma's sweet sounds, and were still all smiles when the waitress arrived with their food. "A hearty breakfast for a happy family," she said in a sing-song voice, placing the plates of eggs, sausage and biscuits before them. "Anything else you need?"

"No, thank you," Sam said.

"It looks good enough to eat," Blake quipped and grinned, placing a napkin in his lap.

The waitress giggled. "He's a keeper," she glanced at Sam, pointing her thumb at him. "Have a great day, you two, and bring your princess back anytime," she added before sliding the bill onto the table and scurrying off.

Sam cut one bite of sausage and paused with fork and knife in hand. "How old do you think she is?"

"The waitress?" Blake winked. "I daresay a woman's age is not territory I tread into."

"No, silly, I meant Emma." She smiled. "I'm thinking she's two and a half, three months old."

"H'mm." He took a sip of his coffee, looking reflective as he considered her question. "She's fairly tiny. I'd say you're probably right. You'd know better than I would, I'm sure." He shrugged.

Satisfied for the moment, Sam lifted the bite of sausage to her lips before starting in on her eggs. Then she paused again, unable to help the worried look she gave Blake.

"I wonder when Emma is due to eat again? I mean, a baby this age, I can't recall how often they eat." She bit her lip, distressed, not able to think quite clearly. "What about the people who dropped her off? When did they feed her last?"

"Don't fret," he answered authoritatively. "You know as well as I do, babies aren't shy about that sort of thing. She'll let you know when she's hungry." He turned to the baby. "Won't you, Princess?"

No sooner were the words out of his mouth than Emma whimpered. In seconds, her whimper mounted to a wail.

"Case in point." He gave Sam a sage-like grin. Then he reached into the diaper bag setting next to him and took out a bottle before unbuckling Emma from her seat.

"I can do it," Sam offered, anxious for any excuse to hold the soft, sweet-smelling bundle in her arms again.

"Nonsense," Blake replied, already settling Emma into the crook of his arms. "You need to eat. Get nourished. You have a long day ahead of you."

"Are you sure—do you know how to feed a baby?" Sam asked hesitantly though she didn't know why. Blake looked completely adept, totally comfortable with Emma nestled against him, already sucking on the bottle. They seemed a natural pair.

"Do I know how to feed a baby . . ." He rolled his eyes at her mockingly. "They didn't give me the 'best uncle in the world' award for nothing. Or was that the universe?" he added, his eyes shining impishly. "Yes, I believe the award included the entire universe."

Sam met his eyes and laughed. "The universe and beyond to unknown galaxies, I'm sure."

"Besides," his eyes held hers as he stared at her intently, "as I told you, I've studied females for some time
now. I happen to know exactly what they like."

His words sent a heated flush up Sam's neck, leaving
a crimson blush on her cheeks. Though she knew she
shouldn't be having such thoughts, watching Blake cuddle Emma she couldn't help but think what it would be
like to be held in his capable arms. Snuggled up to him.
Pressed against his chest.

"Of course," Blake broke the intensity of the moment,
"your job comes next. Because what goes in, must
come—"

"Out." She mustered up a wry grin.

Sam finished eating, then sipped coffee while watching Blake feed Emma. After every couple of ounces,
he'd gently lay the baby over his shoulder and pat her
back to burp her. When the last of the bottle was gone,
he rubbed her back soothingly till she appeared to drift
off to sleep.

He turned his body slightly so Sam could get a view
of Emma's face.

"Are her eyes closed?" he asked softly.

Sam nodded. "You *do* have a way with women, don't
you? Put them right to sleep," she teased.

"Ah, now, is that nice? After I let you eat your breakfast in peace?"

"I'm beginning to know you better than that, Mr.
Dawson. You wouldn't have traded Emma for eggs for
anything, would you?"

His lips curled into a lopsided grin. He turned his torso

so that Emma was facing Sam again. "She is rather sweet, isn't she?"

"Very," Sam replied wistfully.

They sat silent for a while, glowing in the contentment of the moment. It was minutes before reality set in and Sam spoke.

"I know you're right." She sighed, settling the coffee cup back on the saucer.

"Right?" He looked at her, perplexed. "Right about what? I didn't say anything."

"I need to go to the authorities about this, don't I?"

"Did I say something to make you think—?"

"No," she shook her head. "You've been great about it. But I know that's what you're thinking. Legal mind and all." She swallowed hard, twisting her hands together unconsciously. "It's just that," her voice quaked, "I really do think someone meant for me to have her. To have Emma. It's not like I found her in a dingy alley. Someone brought her to my house, all warm and toasty, with bottles and diapers and pacifiers."

As she sat feeling bewildered, Blake's free hand came down over hers possessively, feeling strong . . . warm . . . protective. The strength of his touch shielding her heart, steadying her thoughts.

"I think so, too, Sam. I think someone wants you to have Emma. Knows that you're just the right person for her. But as you know, it's a bit more complicated than that." He stroked her hand soothingly with his thumb. "If you go to the authorities now, and do things the correct way, then no one can come after you later."

He squeezed her fingers with a firm yet intimate assuredness, leaving her no doubt how much he cared. "I'll be there for you if you want me to be. Whatever the two of you need, okay?"

"Thank you." She managed a weak smile though her eyes felt pricked with tears.

"You need to be strong, Sam," he said matter-of-factly.

Looking at Emma who had suddenly begun to wrestle around on Blake's shoulder, she knew she wanted to be. "I will be," she said with resolve.

"Actually, you need to be strong right now. This very minute." He made a sour face as he held up the fussing baby, ready to relinquish her to Sam's care. "Because, my dear lady, it's your turn."

Sam realized what he was up to and instantly the despair faded, and a wry grin burst across her face.

Slipping out of the booth, she stood up, taking Emma from his arms into hers. She narrowed her eyes at him. "Oh, sure. You'll be there, all right. Whatever we need. 'Till it's time for a diaper change."

He winked at her devilishly as he loaded her up with the diaper bag. "I think you'll be needing this." He slipped the bag's strap over her free shoulder.

"See, he really is a rogue," she said to Emma loudly enough for Blake to hear as she and the baby headed toward the restroom.

But she knew it was just his way of making her smile. And she was grateful for that. Grateful for him.

Chapter Five

Blake was right. It had turned out to be a long day, and it wasn't over yet.

Usually at this time of the evening, she would be coming home from the agency, kicking off her heels, and changing into her sweats. Ready to eat dinner, relax for the evening, her day would be done for the most part.

Instead here she was, sitting on the sofa in the quiet of her family room with a snoozing baby girl nestled on her shoulder. She was still in her work clothes though she'd never made it to the agency, and she hadn't given a single thought as to what to fix herself for supper.

Still . . . with Emma's head cradled against her neck, her wet lips brushing her skin, her little feet dangling over her heart, Sam gazed out the window, watching the fading sunset, feeling oddly and totally content.

And, yes, she had to admit, she did feel somewhat tired too. But a good kind of tired.

She and Blake had run errands with Emma, and picked up all kinds of baby paraphernalia. Diapers, formula, bot-

tle liners, clothes, blankets and just as important, a miniature teddy bear that played a sweet-sounding lullaby,
perfect to cuddle up to.

Then there were phone calls to make to her aunt and
uncle, and a call to check in with April. Meanwhile,
Blake made some calls to locate the very best pediatrician in town, and after explaining the situation, made an
appointment for Emma the next day.

After all that, they'd saved the worst till last. The
dreaded trip to the Somersby police station.

Although for all of her anxiety, Sam reflected, the encounter with the police hadn't turned out as badly as she
had anticipated. Chief Tom McKnight readily agreed
with her, in fact. He believed the circumstances sur-
rounding the "drop off," as he kept referring to Emma,
pretty much indicated that someone wanted Sam to have
this child.

It was all too pat, too planned. The timing, the fore-
thought that went into packing the diaper bag, the fact
that the baby was warm and physically cared for up to
the last minute she was placed on Sam's doorstep. It was
definitely premeditated, not a random incident. Sam
didn't seem to be a random choice.

Yet even considering all of that, there still needed to
be an investigation. Checks made on all hospitals in the
tri-state area to see if any babies were missing. Bulletins
put out on the news stations asking for any clues as to
the origin of the baby.

For Sam, it was mind-boggling to think what information might turn up in the next few days, and what
repercussions might ensue from the investigation. But it
was too overwhelming to think about at the moment.

She simply felt lucky that Somersby's chief of police

didn't see anything wrong with her caring for Emma since she was "in the business" anyway. She wanted to enjoy every minute with the darling baby that she could, praying of course, that those minutes would go on forever.

The phone rang as she sat in the dimming room. The sound seemed to be a million miles away, though it caused Emma to stir.

"Shhh . . . it's okay," Sam said softly, quietly, rubbing the small of Emma's back in a soothing circular motion.

She made no motion to get up and answer the phone. At this time of evening, it was probably a telemarketer anyway. Ultimately, they'd just hang up without leaving a message.

"Samantha . . ." She heard a familiar voice say when the answering machine picked up. "I tried to get a hold of you earlier today."

Prescott!

April had told her that he'd called the agency about noon, but Sam had forgotten to call him back. Well, not forgotten really.

For some reason it seemed easy—joyous actually—to call Uncle Dom and Aunt Maria and even April to tell them about Emma. But Prescott? Telling her fiancé that a little baby girl had come into their lives didn't seem like something she should blurt out over the phone. A baby she was seriously considering keeping if the investigation played out right.

"I didn't receive your customary phone call today. And you didn't return my call to you. Should I be getting the impression that you might be angry about something?" He paused as if he expected her to answer. "Perhaps the pre-nuptial agreement?" He paused again.

The pre-nuptial agreement?

It seemed like another lifetime ago that she'd thought about that. Though she'd started out her morning distraught over it, now it seemed like some vague annoyance from her distant past.

"With the family business, it is a necessity, Samantha. True, I should have warned you about it, but—" He paused, his voice questioning. "Samantha, are you there? Where have you been all day, anyway?"

Steadily as she could, she rose from the couch trying not to disturb Emma. Ambling into the kitchen, she picked up the cordless phone from its cradle on the wall.

"Prescott . . . I'm here," she whispered.

"Samantha? Why are you whispering? Do you have laryngitis?"

"No, I have—" *A sleeping baby on my shoulder?* That didn't seem like the best thing to say. "Prescott, I think you should come over. We need to talk," she said in a hushed voice.

"Talk? Can't we talk on the phone? I'm having dinner with mother at eight o'clock."

Oh, yes, Genevieve. The other woman in his life!

"Would you mind stopping by beforehand, Prescott?" she asked as kindly as she could. "It really is important."

"You can't tell me over the phone?"

"I'd rather talk to you in person, if you don't mind. Besides, I haven't seen you since the weekend." *Don't you miss me?* she almost added.

"I would've seen you last night if you hadn't disappointed mother by canceling out on the Aronoff fundraiser. It was a wonderful event."

"I'm sorry about that. I'm sure it was."

There was a distancing silence between them.

"Should I expect you?" she asked tentatively.

"I can come for a few minutes, Samantha," he told her in a tired voice, sounding like a weary parent talking to an insolent child.

"I'll see you soon then." Her stomach churned as she replaced the phone.

Emma shifted positions on her shoulder, and she kissed the baby's head before reluctantly carrying her over to the carrier seat. Sam needed to get something of substance to eat. An encounter with her fiancé required all the fortification she could get.

"I only have a few minutes, Samantha," Prescott told her the precise moment she opened the door. Dressed in his khakis, a light blue button-down and a navy blazer it was obvious he and Genevieve were in for an evening of casual dining.

"You've already mentioned that, Prescott." Her body suddenly felt heavy with dread. Seeing his face, being next to him again, she realized that the chance of him understanding what was going on in her life was fairly non-existent.

For a moment, she fought the impulse to close the door and pretend the bell had never rung. "Come on in," she said instead.

"I see you haven't finished painting the entry yet," he said, referring to the faux finish she'd started a few weeks earlier. "I told you I can hire someone to do it for you. A professional," he offered. "I'm happy to pay for it."

"That's kind of you. But I enjoy doing it," she told him, gazing at the walls, recalling the fulfilling sensation she'd gotten from learning the new creative ragging technique. "I just haven't had time to finish it lately. Besides," she added as she led him into the family room where Emma sat curled up in her pink-cushioned seat, "some things are more important than that."

"Finishing what you start is important, Samantha," he clipped.

She didn't respond to his maxim, letting it hang in the air. There were other things on her mind. Such as, how to introduce Prescott to Emma. Like a video camera set to fast forward, a couple of scenarios played out in her head. Finally, she opted for the direct approach.

"Prescott, I want you to meet Emma." She pointed to the carrier sitting on the floor with baby Emma snuggled inside. Prescott squinted down his nose at the sight.

"Emma?" he responded blankly. "Emma who?"

At his mention of her name, Emma's little eyes shot open. Her fists flung up into the air, and she began to pout. Immediately, Sam swooped down to unbuckle the seat. Cradling Emma in her arms, she paced the length of the room, cooing and calming the squirming, startled baby.

Even though Prescott looked less than thrilled to be standing there watching her, Sam's heart swooned. Holding Emma felt so deliciously good and special. She felt so close to the little one. So comfortable with her in her arms, seeming like they'd always been a part of each others' lives. It was hard to believe she'd only known the precious little girl since this morning.

"Actually, I don't know Emma's last name." Sam deliberately fussed over Emma's sleeper, straightening it on her torso, anything to avoid eye contact with her fiancé at the moment. "In fact, Emma isn't really her first name. It's just a name that—" *that Blake and I agreed*

on this morning. Because I didn't think he should con-
tinue telling the world her name was Princess.

The thought formed an involuntary smile on Sam's
lips, but she tried to squelch it. Somehow it didn't seem
wise or even fair to be grinning while Prescott was standing there with a scowl on his face, looking utterly confused.

"It's her name for now," Sam finished the sentence.

"Then this is one of your work cases, I assume?"

"No, Prescott, she isn't. She, uh . . ." She stalled and
halted her pacing. "Would you like to sit down? Can I
get you something to drink?"

The niceties only seemed to annoy Prescott more.
"No, thank you, Samantha. I have to be leaving soon,
remember? I don't want to be late for mother. But you
can tell me what you needed so desperately to talk about.
If it's the pre-nuptial agreement—"

"Actually," she interrupted, nodding to the sweet thing
in her arms, "it's about—Emma." Sam hugged the baby
tightly, protectively against her body, preparing for a
possible onslaught of heated words.

"Okay. Well, tell me then." He glanced at his watch
impatiently. "Does her family need money, a place to
live, what? How much?"

"Not exactly. You see, Emma was dropped off on
my—"

The doorbell rang again cutting off her sentence.
Saved by the bell! she intoned in her head.

"Come in," she yelled out, not really caring who it
might be, welcoming any interruption.

At her invitation, a huge rectangular box walked in
the front door. Actually, it was a man-sized box being

muscled by Blake who peeked around it. Glancing into the family room, he spotted Emma.

"Princess! There's my Princess," he exclaimed, setting the box down.

"The baby belongs to you?" Prescott asked him.

"Oh, no, not at all." Blake held the box steady with one hand, while nonchalantly brushing dust from his herringbone sport coat, black tee shirt and jeans with the other.

"I was at the store purchasing furniture for my office, having just moved to Somersby you see, and low and behold, the strangest of things happened." His eyes widened and Sam detected the teasing look in his eye. "I found myself in a baby furniture store. Isn't that unbelievable?" He addressed his audience, a look of mock incredulity on his face.

"And I knew the little one didn't have a crib to lay down in tonight, do you, sweetheart?" He wriggled his nose at Emma. "So, I didn't think Sam would mind if—"

"Sam?" Prescott questioned, apparently noting the warm familiarity in Blake's voice. "You mean *Samantha?*" He flapped back the sides of his blazer, placing his hands on his hips over a cordovan belt. "Samantha, do you know this person?" he questioned her, though his eyes remained steady on Blake.

Before she could muster an answer, Blake stuck out his free hand in an attempt to shake hands. "You must be Prescott Sterling."

Prescott ignored Blake's outstretched hand. "You know me? We know each other?"

"No, we've never met. I guessed you were Sterling from the monogram on your shirt pocket." Blake nodded at the other man's puffed out chest. "And from the black BMW out front—the PRES IV on the license plates."

"And you are—?" Prescott glared at Blake.

"Blake Dawson." Once again, Blake attempted a handshake but his effort was rejected. "I'm—"

"An old friend of the family," Uncle Dominic's voice piped up as he and Aunt Maria practically skipped in the door carrying armloads of over-sized shopping bags.

"Oh, Sam, honey," Aunt Maria bubbled over, holding up a bag in each hand. "I found the most adorable crib bumper and quilt set. And sheets and blankets with the cutest lambs on them. I hope you like them. But if you don't, I'll be glad to take them back. Not a problem."

Her aunt dropped the bags where she stood in the entryway. Suddenly they seemed to take a back seat to what she truly had on her mind. She sailed into the family room, greeted Prescott with barely a glance, and rushed over to where Sam stood holding the baby. "Oh, there she is," Aunt Maria gushed, "baby Emma."

Prescott glowered at Sam. "But I thought you said her name wasn't Emma."

"Well, they can't go on calling her Princess," Uncle Dom spoke up, snickering jovially as he helped Blake prop the cumbersome box against the wall. "B.D. told me the whole story, Sam."

"B.D. who?" Prescott snapped.

Sensing her fiancé's irritation, Sam looked over at him. She was right. Everything about his body language was grim and stern, from his locked jaw to his stiff legs.

She realized she'd never really seen him this way. Of course, she'd never given him any reason to be annoyed with her either. She'd always gone along with his wishes, with Genevieve's whims.

"I'd like to hear the entire story, too, Samantha. I have three minutes," he said tersely. "Will that be enough?"

"Let's go into the kitchen," she replied softly to Prescott, settling the baby into her aunt's open arms. "Will you excuse us?" She turned to the collective group in the room.

As she and Prescott made their exit, she could feel Blake's eyes seeking hers out, following her every step.

Strange, she thought, *after just one day, I feel as naturally drawn to him as I do to Emma.*

She wouldn't allow herself to look at him, though. Knew she couldn't return his gaze. Already they seemed to know each other so well. Too well. If she looked into his eyes, she was certain he'd be able to read her every thought.

If he saw any inkling of the feelings she had toward him, he might mistake it for something else. If he saw distress in her eyes, he might try to come to her rescue. Either way could be uncomfortable where Prescott was concerned.

Working to maintain a blank expression, she led her vexed fiancé into the kitchen.

"Samantha." Prescott's tone was unforgiving. "You tell me the baby's name is Emma. Then you say it's not. You tell me we have to talk. But you really haven't said anything. And everyone else—including that Blake person—seems to know what's going on. Care to explain?"

His hands were still on his hips, and Sam was still trying to find a way to make their tête-a-tête more comfortable.

"Care to sit down?" she asked for the second time that evening, motioning at an antique oak chair.

"I'll stand," he replied firmly, moving his arms from

his waist and crossing them over his chest. "I'm running out of time, Samantha."

And patience, he may as well have added, Sam thought. Though she couldn't really blame him.

She folded her arms defensively around herself, too. "The truth is, someone dropped a baby girl on my porch this morning. A baby girl without a name. I named her Emma because there was a waitress who—well, never mind that." She waved her hands, dismissing the explanation. "The whole drop," she said, using the chief of police's term, "seemed to be totally premeditated. I don't think it was compulsive. I think someone thought long and hard about it and chose me. The police think so, too."

Prescott seemed to heave a sigh of relief. "So you *have* contacted the police?"

"Yes." She nodded, noticing that the news appeared to make his arms relax some, the air about him seemed to thaw. "They're already conducting an investigation to try to locate Emma's—the baby's—parents. But so far, there are few clues. And it might turn out that her parents are never found." She couldn't help the sparkle of hope she felt at the thought.

"And you look happy about that for some reason." Prescott lifted his brow, meaning he required further explanation.

"Well . . . I mean . . . if there's no one else . . . if no parent comes forward . . ." she stammered. "I want to have her, Prescott. I want to raise Emma. And if it all works out that way, wouldn't it be wonderful?" She could feel herself gleaming involuntarily.

"Samantha." He was using his parent-to-child tone again. "Have you ever considered what kind of people leave babies on strangers' doorsteps? Typically drug addicts or worse," he warned. "It's not a stray cat that you take in off the street and keep."

Sam clenched her teeth, trying desperately to keep her voice calm. Trying to find some sort of reason to still love him.

"You're right, Prescott. *It* is not a stray. *It* is a baby girl. A delicate human being. A brand new life in need of nurturing, care, and love. And if the parents are not found, if no one else is going to be there for her, I want to give her all those things. And I will."

Shocked. She could tell her words had shocked him, and she felt badly about it. Possibly he was as stunned as she'd been yesterday when she received the pre-nuptial agreement.

"Mother always warned me you had a wayward predilection for those kind of . . ."

"For those kind of what?" Sam urged him to finish his thought though she already knew the answer. *For those kind of people* . . . she could practically hear Genevieve's condescending voice say the words.

"Never mind, Samantha. The point is, you never consulted me about this."

"I know, Prescott. There was so much to do today. And I didn't want to tell you over the phone. But that's what I'm trying to do right now." She placed her hand on his arm affectionately. "I'm trying to consult you. To tell you that if you'll just look into that baby's eyes, if you'll just hold her in your arms, you'll see how right it feels. I promise you." She pleaded him with her eyes, tried to coax him with her touch.

But he shrugged out from under the caress of her hand, retrieving a ring of keys from the pocket of his blazer.

"I don't know what's gotten into you, Samantha. But you're not thinking rationally about this." He rattled the keys at her. "Plot it out like you usually do. You'll see it doesn't make sense." He shook his head, obviously disappointed in her. "You're not thinking with a clear head. Not acting like yourself."

"I apologize, Prescott. I know this has been a lot to spring on you," she answered him sincerely. "And you're right. I'm not thinking with a clear head. Not a totally clear head. I'm also thinking with my heart." She paused, her uncle's words echoing in her mind. *You have a good mind and a caring heart . . .*

"But you're also wrong," she told him. "And maybe I've been wrong, too. I *am* acting like myself. I know it. This morning when I discovered Emma, when I held her in my arms, I rediscovered the real me."

Chapter Six

"Blake, you didn't have to, you know." Sam turned to face him from the passenger seat of his car.

The fresh, intoxicating scent of lily-of-the-valley cologne . . . the sweet aroma of baby powder . . . both filled the car, wreaking havoc on his brain. He tried to shake his senses free of the pleasurable mix of scents long enough to focus on her words. But he was like a lost puppy in a field of tall, delicious-smelling flowers.

"Didn't have to?" He glanced over at her, noticing that her hair looked truly golden, highlighted by the October morning sun that shone through the car window. *Didn't have to what? Find the closeness of her so gratifying? The scent of her so appealing?*

"Drive us."

"Oh, yes, that." He straightened in the seat, gripping the steering wheel more tightly. "Well, I'm the one who made the phone calls and opted for the pediatrician halfway across town. I felt it was the only gentlemanly thing to do." *And all I wanted to do.*

"It's very nice of you, but you've done so much already."

"Considering you're my only client to date, what else would I be doing at this time of the day?" He chuckled and leveled his eyes on her momentarily.

She was gazing out the windshield and sounded wistful as she spoke, "You've helped me shop for all her things. Went to the police station with me. Bought her crib and wouldn't let me repay you. Then even set it up." She seemed to be enumerating his good deeds in her mind, which was fine by him. "You've really gone beyond the call of duty."

Then as if seeing something troubling in the distance, she turned to him suddenly, a concerned expression shadowing her face. "Really, maybe you need to ease up. What if you get burned out on us before Emma has her first birthday? There will be no one to come to her birthday party except for Uncle Dom and Aunt Maria."

He laughed at that, and reached over to pat her hands. "Sam. Don't talk like that. You'll give the poor child some psychological affliction." Catching a glimpse of Emma in the back seat, all snug in her knit cap and one piece zip-up, he made a promise to her over his shoulder, "Don't fret, Little One, I'll be there."

Part of him wanted to warn Sam not to think about the future as she seemed to be. After all, who even knew what the next few days would hold? The police could track down the baby's parents any minute. Or the parents could have a change of heart.

But, he didn't say anything. How could he? It would be so hypocritical of him since he found himself imagining the future, too. A future with Sam and Emma.

Perhaps it was foolish. Actually, there was no 'perhaps'

involved. It was downright ludicrous. But last night helping Sam put sheets on the crib mattress . . . having Chinese take-out with her, Dom, Maria and little Emma curled in his lap . . . things seemed perfect. Perfectly natural. Like a scene that had always been . . . and always would be.

And this morning when he woke up, he couldn't help himself. His first thoughts were of Sam and Emma, filling him with a lightness and a strange kind of happiness like he'd never experienced.

Sam and Emma. He felt more at home with them in a matter of a couple of days than he had ever felt with any woman he'd dated back in Boston.

"Why *did* you leave Boston?" Sam asked, interrupting his thoughts. Actually, she seemed to have read them. "Why did you come to Somersby?"

"Ah, well. I'd visited your uncle here a few years ago," he told her. "Probably before you moved back," he replied, noting the confused look on her face. "I instantly found the burg appealing. The drive-in. The corner drugstore. The boutiques. It's an interesting combination of small town Americana with an artsy feel mixed in," he added, wondering if things would've been different between them if they'd crossed paths years ago.

"Not to say that Boston isn't a great city. And manageable, too. But as a partner in an extremely prestigious firm there, soon I grew disenchanted with the firm's corporate workings, the pressures of the limelight. It didn't suit me. And after a while, I didn't suit the firm. They especially didn't appreciate the pro bono work I was doing on the side."

"You'd think they'd look at it as good public relations." Her forehead creased as she spoke. She always seemed so concerned and interested. Was that her way with everyone, he wondered?

"Yes, *you* would think that," he said, complimenting her business instincts. "But it took away time from wealthy, billable clients."

"Do you plan to do pro bono work here in Somersby?"

He inclined his head toward her and nodded. "Hopefully, I can do some good here. But it's not one-sided. Somersby will be good for me, too, I think."

"A social worker at heart, huh?" Her admiring eyes . . . her laudatory smile. It was all the praise he needed to warm him. But he responded otherwise, giving her a cocky look and a sideways grin.

"Fair maiden, you forget my heritage. By nature I'm supposed to be reserved. Unfeeling. And a scoundrel. You'll ruin my reputation with such talk." He quirked an eyebrow her way, teasing more. "Are you the only woman in America who never watched *Sense & Sensibility*? Don't you know the first thing about us cold-hearted Brits?"

She laughed, the sound delighting him. "I'm sure April has. I'll have to ask her for the inside scoop. Maybe she knows something about knaves disguised in white shining armor."

"We're a dangerous, shifty lot." He grinned.

Once their banter subsided, he spotted her fidgeting hands from the corner of his eye.

"You're nervous," he said, stating the obvious.

"Yes." She took a deep breath, rubbing her fingers anxiously. "I'm uneasy about what the pediatrician will say. I've never been such a worrier. It's hard to explain. But I hope Emma is healthy and well-nourished and normal and her development is—"

"Whoa, hold on there." How badly he wished he could take her hand, intertwine her fingers with his, give her the strength and calm she needed at the moment.

"She's beautiful and wonderful," he told her soothingly. "Everything will be fine with her, Sam. I'm sure of it."

At least he was sure until a moment passed, and suddenly her concerns caught up with him, stirring him to worry, too. "And if anything is wrong, which I don't believe there is," he added for good measure when she looked at him fretfully, "we'll make it right. Whatever it takes. Agreed?"

She nodded, her blue eyes glistening with appreciation. "Oh, I forgot to tell you. Before I went to bed last night, I was cleaning out the diaper bag and found a typed list of the immunizations she's received so far."

"Any doctor or birthdate?"

She shook her head disconsolately. Was that a tear welling up in her eye?

"She doesn't have a birthday."

Combined with her earlier comment, it was clear to him that Sam was stressing over Emma's first birthday. It seemed terribly important for her to resolve the matter.

"Of course she does. We'll see how old the pediatrician thinks she is, and then we'll give her a birthdate, all right?" Then to lighten the moment, he added, "I'm thinking she's a Leo. Strong-willed and cute as a kitten."

She smiled up at him, but maintained her focus. "And we'll give her a first birthday party?"

"She'll have a party," he agreed. *Though Sterling will be there . . . and you'll be married to him by that time.* He didn't want to remind her—or himself, for that matter.

"How did the old boy take it last night? The news?"

Perhaps instinctively, Sam knew to whom he was referring. "About as well as I took the news about the prenup."

"Ah." He glanced over giving her his best grimace, and then his most consoling glance. But neither expression was at all sincere.

How can I feel so pleased about Sterling's reaction when the dear girl is obviously so pained by it? I truly am a scoundrel at heart!

He'd found himself pleased last night, too, when he saw the engaged couple part company with neither a kiss nor a hug. Sam hadn't even walked Sterling to her front door, but rather lagged behind in the kitchen.

"He'll get accustomed to the idea," he tried to reassure her, though it was the last thing on the list he wanted to see happen. "It's a bit much to heap on someone all at once, I suppose."

"Maybe . . ." her voice trailed off.

She turned and glanced out the car window, her comment leaving room for doubt.

And hope.

Sam found the décor of the pediatrician's office quite pleasing, the seaside motif and aquamarine hues both relaxing and delightful. Apparently, the younger set thought so too. Two toddlers stood in front of the walled-in six-foot-long aquarium filled with brightly-colored tropical fish, their eyes wide with wonder. A preteen girl sat in a wicker rocker beneath an imitation palm tree, sniffling and sneezing, her stuffy head buried in a book.

After checking in with the receptionist, Sam joined

Blake and Emma who were sitting in some cushioned chairs splattered with a design of palm fronds. Blake held Emma on his lap, talking to her about the fish which, of course, she was far too young to focus on. Still, that he was attempting to teach Emma about her world was endearing and the tone of his voice pleasant to listen to.

Periodically, a nurse would appear at the door leading back to the examining rooms, and call out a child's name. But when it was their turn to be called back, no child's name was mentioned. The disparity tugged at Sam's heart.

"Would you like to come back now?" The redheaded nurse looked directly at Sam, then at Blake.

Sam nodded, turning to Blake with a wan smile. He seemed to know what she was thinking without her having to voice it.

"She has us," is all he said.

His words were insightful, his nearness comforting, making Sam wonder about herself . . . and him.

How had this happened so quickly, after all? Where had this connection come from?

Several days ago, she didn't know Blake Dawson existed on earth. And now she looked to him for consolation . . . smiles . . . ease of mind. She marveled at their immediate closeness. Enjoyed their silly banter. And wanted to share everything about Emma with him.

Obviously, Blake felt the same bond too. At least she knew he did where Emma was concerned. Walking down the hallway to the exam room, he held the wide-eyed baby over his head, cooing and chuckling at her with every step he took. No one would ever suspect he wasn't the child's father. His every action was so loving, his eyes so full of pleasure.

The nurse settled their threesome in an exam room, and a minute or so later, the pediatrician walked in, eyes downcast skimming a chart.

"Samantha Stevenson? Blake Dawson?" She glanced up from the file folder and greeted them, extending her hand. "I'm Dr. Farrell. Meredith Farrell."

"Nice to meet you." Sam shook her hand, glad that the doctor's smile was as warm and friendly as her touch.

"And it appears you have your hands full." The middle-aged doctor turned to Blake, seeming to notice the cozy fit Emma made in his arms. "You're Blake Dawson? And this is Baby Doe, I assume?"

"This is little Emma," Blake said fondly, holding the baby up for Dr. Farrell to see.

"Her name is Emma?" Confused, the doctor glanced back at the chart then at Sam who was already shaking her head.

"No, we just thought, well, we thought that—"

Dr. Farrell held up her hand, halting Sam's stammering explanation. "I understand. May I?" The doctor held out her arms to Blake.

"Emma, the nice doctor is going to give you an examination which is a rather large, cumbersome word meaning she's going to look you over and make sure you're perfectly fine." He placed the baby in the doctor's arms who chuckled softly at his explanation.

"Oh, now. Aren't you a beautiful girl?" Dr. Farrell looked down on the bundle in her arms, patting the baby's bottom soothingly as she walked over to the examining table and laid Emma down gently.

Hearing the words and the doctor's kind tone made Sam liked Dr. Farrell even more. Yes, they'd definitely made the right choice in pediatricians. Well, at least

Blake had. Glancing over, she smiled her thanks to him. He grinned back, his eyes telling her that he was thinking the same thing. And just to make sure she knew, he reached over and patted her knee understandingly.

After unsnapping Emma's sleeper, Dr. Farrell's hands moved over the baby adeptly, testing limbs, counting toes, pressing fingertips over organs, weighing and measuring, taking her temperature.

"Hard to imagine anyone could give her up, isn't it?" she said almost to herself as her hands continued to probe. "But at least whoever did leave her on your doorstep did the right thing for her. And from what you told us, she's had her first series of immunizations, which is a good thing."

Dr. Farrell changed Emma's diaper before snapping up the soft flannel sleeper around her small body again. "We'll use the soiled diaper for a urine sample," she told them as she sat with one hip on the examining table, cradling Emma in her arms once more. "But I'm assuming the albumin tests will come back normal. From my observations, I'm happy to say it seems you have a very healthy little girl here. Thirteen pounds, six ounces."

Like an expectant father who had just witnessed the final moments of childbirth, Blake exhaled a deep sigh of relief. It surprised Sam, who thought the man was always totally in control and had nothing but optimistic thoughts.

He must have been more worried than he'd let on, she thought, and this time she reached over and patted his knee consolingly.

"Thank you, doctor," he said, raking his fingers through his thick hair. "Thank you very much."

"No reason to thank me. I'm always glad to be the

bearer of good news." She smiled at them. "However, Emma will be needing more immunizations in the next month or so. She'll require the second oral polio, another DPT immunization the following month, and more boosters in the months to follow. But the nurse will go over those dates with you."

She looked back and forth between them. "Do you have any questions? Anything I can help you with? It must be a rather difficult situation to be faced with."

"Not really," Blake spoke up. "She's such a delightful baby. But I do think there's one thing we've both been wondering about."

The doctor looked at him expectantly, waiting for his question. Sam flashed him a puzzled look, not sure what he was about to say.

Before he spoke, he seemed to make a purposeful act of reaching out and covering Sam's hand with his, bonding them to the moment and their unified concern for Emma.

"Is there any way . . . what I mean is . . ." he grappled for words. "Can you tell us how old Emma is?" As he looked Dr. Farrell in the eye, his hand tightened around Sam's.

Tilting her head, the doctor spoke softly, sympathetically. "Obviously, I can't tell you the exact day she was born, and I wish I could. I know that's very important to many people. But there are certain factors that allow me to give you a good estimate of her age if you'd like."

"Like the immunizations?" Sam asked, her voice sounding nervous even to herself.

The doctor nodded. "Assuming they were given at the proper times, which at this point, I believe they were. But also, Emma seems to be in what we call the Phase

II stage of development which occurs between six and fourteen weeks.

"Actually, from all indications—her coordination of behavior, grasping motions, constant smiles—she appears to be in the latter weeks of the stage. I'd say Emma is anywhere from eleven to thirteen weeks, approximately three months old."

"Let's see, here we are at the third week of October. September. August." Blake counted backwards. "That makes it the last week of July or so." He turned to Sam with a wink. "Didn't I tell you I sensed Leo personality traits? Do I know my females or what?"

Both women chuckled at that and even Emma's cherubic face lit up with a smile. But Sam still had other concerns.

"Dr. Farrell," she started out haltingly, "I realize Emma's only a baby, but being abandoned by her mother . . . I've seen so many cases, so much emotional scarring. Is there any way to prevent it?"

The doctor bit her lip, seemingly considering her answer. "I'm not a child psychologist so I can't give you any statistics. And my answer may sound flippant, but I'm going to say it anyway. I'm with the Beatles on this one."

"Excuse me?" Sam was puzzled.

"Excellent Liverpool chaps," Blake quipped in his thickest accent. "Smart woman."

The pediatrician looked down at the child in her arms before speaking to Sam and Blake. Her voice held a sweet seriousness. "I believe all this baby needs is love. And it's apparent you two have much of that to offer. The way you look at each other. Interact. Comfort one another. And care about her . . ." She paused.

"All I can say is, if the parents aren't found, and when the two of you marry," she nodded at the ring on Sam's finger, "if you should decide to adopt Emma, she'd be very lucky and very loved. And what else," she asked the couple as she handed Emma back to Blake, "does a little girl need to grow up into a beautiful young woman?"

Chapter Seven

Sam glanced up from the computer monitor on her desk. Gazing at the new addition to the corner of her office, a satisfied smile crossed her lips.

April had borrowed a small portable playpen from her older sister and set it up in Sam's office. Emma lay inside it, staring at the butterfly mobile that hung from the side, her tiny limbs moving excitedly, the sound of her Pampers rustling in the quiet of the room.

The porta-pen seemed like the perfect set-up for the next week or so until Sam could start interviewing nanny candidates. And, what was even better, none of the agency's other employees appeared to mind the baby's presence.

In fact, her co-workers seemed thrilled to have Emma there. She was a novelty, a bright spot in everyone's day. She gave them something to smile about, a diversion from the pressing, unpleasant issues they normally dealt with. She was a positive symbol of what their jobs were all about.

However, there was one problem, Sam thought, grinning to herself. Namely, she wasn't sure how much work she'd actually accomplish in the next few days. Not because of Emma—but because of her co-workers who kept peeking their heads in her office door every ten minutes or so. Everyone wanted to get to know the abandoned baby girl, wanted to make silly faces at her, talk a little baby talk, or hold her in their arms. And who could blame them?

"Come in," she called out cheerily, not at all surprised to hear yet another knock on her door.

However, the visitor did surprise her.

"Blake!"

"Good day, ladies." He blew a kiss in the direction of Emma's playpen. "Lovely ladies, I might add."

He fixed his dancing eyes on Sam, and though she knew better than to mistake his casual compliment for anything more than innate British charm, his coltish stare made her flush with warmth.

"Everyone well this morning?" he asked her, inclining his head toward Emma. "How did it go last night? Sleep well?"

"I missed you," she said.

No, she hadn't exactly 'said' the words. She had blurted them out—without even thinking. How must she have sounded? Totally flirtatious? Coquettish? He mentioned sleep . . . and she replied she missed him. How embarrassing!

"I mean, uh, we missed you," she stammered. "Emma and I."

Oh, great! Now she sounded like a helpless female. Someone who needed him. Depended on him. Was desperate and couldn't get along without him for an entire evening.

But truth be told . . . she *had* missed him, and she wished he had stopped by last night.

As she sat in the rocker feeding Emma the previous evening, she felt the same quiet peacefulness she had experienced the night before. But in her heart she sensed something wasn't quite the same. There seemed to be something missing, a slight void. It wasn't until Emma let out one very loud, unladylike burp that Sam heard her own laughter echo in the empty rooms of her house and realized what "it" was. It wasn't a "something" at all. It was a "someone."

Blake.

Blake would've shared the funny sweetness of the moment with her, his deep, full-hearted laugh resounding along with hers. Or he would've screwed up that handsomely carved face of his into an exaggerated scowl, making her laugh even more.

And later, while Emma lay in her crib sleeping—the crib that Blake had bought for her—Sam looked in on the baby and found herself thinking of the Englishman once more.

She knew he would have appreciated the endearing specialness of the moment, seeing Emma's adorable little body content at rest. He would have understood the preciousness of the scene in just the same way he seemed to understand everything.

Like their trip to the pediatrician. He had made it so easy. He'd offered his unwavering support, hiding his own pensiveness. His sturdy hand holding hers, binding them together for whatever came their way.

She wondered at the sudden attachment and couldn't

make sense of it—until later that night, when Emma cried out, and Sam rushed to her cribside to scoop the baby into her arms and comfort her.

Even with eyes clenched shut, the whimpering baby was blindly soothed by Sam's embrace. Felt at home in Sam's arms. It didn't matter that Sam wasn't her mother and didn't share the same blood in her veins. The trust— the bond—was still there. Unquestionably, in an instant.

Just as it was with Blake. Like a gift sent from some- where—the heavens, who knew?—some place outside of themselves where the best laid plans and charts and lists have no place, that's where he seemed to have come from. And the attachment . . . the attraction . . . the bond was instantaneous. Though totally inexplicable, unfath- omably perplexing, it existed, strong and real.

"I missed you, too," she heard him reply through the haziness of her thoughts. However, he bent over to pick up Emma from the playpen as he spoke, and Sam couldn't be sure if he was addressing her or the baby.

After he smoothed the ruffled collar away from Emma's chin, Sam then watched him feel at the soft fabric covering the baby's feet. "Do you think this sleeper is getting a bit small?" He eyed the pink and white striped outfit.

"Small? It wasn't too small when I put it on her this morning. She can probably get another week or two's wear out of it."

"Don't we want her to be able to stretch and grow to a formidable height? After all," he cocked his head con- templatively, "she could grow up to be the first female president—or at least the next governor."

Sam chuckled at him. "I don't think the sleeper is going to hinder her growth or her gubernatorial chances."

"One never knows. Don't they bind babies feet in other cultures? To make them smaller?"

"Maybe in the dark ages," she quipped.

Blake unconsciously patted the baby's bottom as he spoke. "I've been meaning to stop at the department store anyway. Perhaps I'll pick up a few new outfits for her."

Sam's eyes narrowed, but her smiled widened. "Shouldn't you be drumming up business instead of buying baby clothes? Don't you have clients to attend to?" She giggled, shaking her head at him and his open fondness for Emma.

"As a matter of fact, I do have some business to attend to. Business with my most beautiful client of all." He winked, letting her know he was speaking of her.

Why did his silly, flirty compliments always make her cheeks tingle with warmth? Cause her heart to feel fluttery in her chest? Make her have to will her voice to sound light and teasing?

"I don't have much competition in that area, considering I'm your only client."

"H'mm . . ." He mused, gazing at the ceiling above them. "Now that I think about it . . . you're right." He chuckled.

Sam pretended to heave a stapler in his direction, but he held up Emma as a protective shield.

"You're lucky you're holding a baby," she told him.

"Let me make it up to you. How about lunch? On the square? It's a perfect fall day. Positively golden."

In the confines of her office, their light-hearted banter seemed innocuous enough. The relationship growing between the two of them—all for Emma's sake, of course—didn't seem objectionable, just natural and right.

More and more, it was as if she existed between two worlds—this one she shared with Emma and Blake, and the one that included Prescott and a looming pre-nuptial agreement. And though she could accept that and deal with it, she wasn't sure she wanted to expose her dual existence on the square at that moment.

"Not only golden," Blake's voice interrupted her thoughts, "but russet and copper, too. We can talk business outside, can't we? Days like this don't come along often," he added temptingly.

Despite her reservations, Sam knew his words were true. Earlier, she had glanced out the window by April's reception desk onto Somersby's grassy square. The glorious sun . . . the mild cool air . . . the swirling leaves in autumn golds and burnt oranges . . . it all appeared inviting, invigorating.

Still . . . it didn't seem altogether proper for an engaged woman to be out in public, in the light of day, having lunch with another man, did it?

Although—did that ring true when the other man was her attorney? And when her fiancé's legal demands had led to their introduction, their time spent together?

And would she feel uncomfortable about accepting Blake's invitation if he weren't so darned good-looking? If she didn't see something curiously special when she looked into his eyes?

"It's almost time for Emma's bottle," she hedged, void of answers for all the questions swirling in her mind.

"And April is prepared to feed her, Sam. Besides, I've already purchased your lunch. It's waiting for you on April's desk."

Her excuses were wearing thin. "How could you? You don't even know what I like," she challenged petulantly.

He gave her a knowing, lopsided grin. "Chicken salad on a croissant. Tomato. Lettuce. No chips. You'd love to eat them, but much too fattening. Kosher pickle. Bottled water. And a bite-sized chocolate mint for dessert."

Incredulous, she felt her jaw go slack, her mouth fall open. She'd been seeing Prescott for two years, and there was no way he'd ever guess so closely.

Reading her face, Blake tsk, tsked. "Dear Ms. Stevenson, when are you ever going to believe me? I know my females."

"So what is it you wanted to talk to me about?"

Sam took a sip of her bottled water and squinted at Blake, wishing she had her sunglasses. Not only to shade her eyes, but also to have something to hide behind in case she spied someone she knew on the square. However, Blake had whisked her out of the office much too quickly to think of minor details like that. She'd barely had time to grab her jean jacket, throw it on over her long khaki skirt, and give Emma a kiss good-bye.

"Let's give it a moment, shall we?" he asked, resting his head on the back of the bench they shared, closing his eyes to soak up the warm rays.

"Ah, feel that sun. Magnificent, isn't it?" He popped an eye open momentarily to address her. "Try it," he urged. "It's rather incredible."

"How can I?" she protested. "You said we needed to talk."

His eyes shut tight again, he droned lazily. "Just pretend you're a cat. A cat with a full stomach. Lazing in the sun. An adorable, furry ball of a creature," his voice drifted off.

Sam laughed at his description. "Okay, I'll try," she

complied. "Except I might need help with the furry ball imagery."

Glancing over at him, she saw the corner of his mouth crimp into a smile. But he kept his eyes closed, appearing peacefully content. It looked so inviting, and suddenly her eyes felt terribly heavy. Getting up several times during the night to attend to a baby quickly took its toll on a person.

Settling her head on the back of the bench next to Blake's, she was more than willing to let the therapeutic rays caress her skin, soothe her mind, rejuvenate her energy. For a moment she was concerned about who might see her lazing there . . . who might spot her with another man. But that was only for a moment. Frankly, she felt too exhausted and the sun felt too delicious on her face . . . so cozy and relaxing, setting her mind to a drifting state.

She and Prescott had shared many times together . . . charity events, fundraisers, dinners. But they had never shared such a pure, simplistic moment like this. They had never shared the sun, had they? She tried to remember. Side by side. No words. All warmth.

In the distance, a young child's cry sounded and Sam's body flinched involuntarily. Automatically. Just as automatic was Blake's touch as he reached out to stroke her leg. "She's fine," he whispered. "She's with April, remember?"

His comforting pats were becoming as familiar as the fresh, tempting masculine scent of him. His closeness natural and right even as he sat now with his legs sprawled out on the bench, his right leg slightly touching her left one. It was hard to believe that when she first spotted him in Uncle Dom's store she thought he came off as brassy and full of himself.

With all that had happened in the past few days, she knew undoubtedly that he was anything but. Just as her uncle had confided, Blake seemed too good to be true. His humor, his gregarious nature, the way he was always there to help her, protect her and—

She shot up abruptly. "You're stalling for a reason, aren't you?" The realization caused a sick churning in her stomach. "It's something awful you need to talk to me about, isn't it?"

As if in slow motion, Blake drew his lean body up from the bench and rubbed at his face before fixing his gaze on her. Suddenly, the look of contentment had disappeared from his eyes, the trace of a smile faded from his lips. Sorrowful concern marked his expression.

Finally he retrieved a piece of paper from his jacket pocket and sighed. "I received this from Sterling's attorneys yesterday. It's an addendum to the pre-nuptial agreement."

"An addendum?"

"It's in regard to Emma, Sam."

She took the paper from his hand and tried to read over the legalese written there. But at the sound of Emma's name, her hands were already shaking, her mind too jumbled with questions and worries to make sense of anything.

"Just tell me, Blake," she pleaded, thrusting the paper back at him. "Don't make me read this. Please."

He took the paper from her and slid it back into his pocket. Then he faced her, his eyes apologetic, looking as if it were his fault he had to deliver upsetting news. "Basically it says that any child who is not a direct

Sterling descendant will never be recognized as a beneficiary of the Sterling fortune or assets," he said, his voice strained but calm, professional.

"In other words, the child may be a Sterling by name, but not by blood and will not be accepted as such. Therefore, he or she shall never be considered an heir."

The words were like a slap in the face. Tears instantly sprung up behind her eyes, indignation and anger welling up inside her.

How could Prescott be so cold? How could he not even take a moment to contact her himself? Was this really how he felt, his decision? Or more of Genevieve's demands?

Did it matter? She finally asked herself. Obviously, the results were the same. Obviously, a baby's life . . . a child's future . . . didn't mean much to him. His bloodline meant much more. He didn't care that the child would grow up to feel like an outsider. Never feeling good enough to be a part of the esteemed Sterling family.

Well, Sam resolved, wiping at the tears staining her cheeks, *I do care*.

"Thanks for the sandwich, Blake," she said stonily, getting up from the bench. "But I should get back to the agency."

He stood up and started to come near her, his arms outstretched, his eyes imploring. But she backed away, too angry and upset at Prescott's latest stunt to settle into the comfort of Blake's arms. And also, far too embarrassed.

What must he think of me, engaged to someone like Prescott? Not much, I guess . . .

"Sam, please wait," he pleaded soothingly. "Let's talk."

But what would I say? How do I explain it? Except say that I'm not the same person I was six months ago when I said "yes" to Prescott. Not even the same person I was a week ago. I met you . . . I found Emma . . . and nothing's quite the same.

"I—I don't know what to say."

"Would you like for me to issue a response to his attorneys?" he asked quietly.

She shook her head sullenly. "Just send me a bill for your time. Forget you were ever involved, okay?"

Then she walked off, leaving behind an empty lunch sack, turning her back on Blake and the positively golden day.

Chapter Eight

B*ut I am involved.*

He'd wanted to shout out the words as she turned and walked away from him. But he didn't. It just didn't seem fair to burden her with his feelings, too. After all, she had enough to handle with baby Emma and Prescott, that idiot fiancé of hers.

As for himself, if he never laid eyes on Sterling again, it would be too soon. True, he fancied himself more a lover than a fighter, but the spoiled millionaire got under his skin. If they should ever cross paths, it'd be tough to restrain himself from going at the bloke. Or to refrain from at least giving the fool a harsh verbal thrashing.

The only way he'd manage to keep his anger in check would be purely out of respect for Sam—because he had no respect for Sterling.

How moronic the man was! Did he think just because he was wealthy he could buy the kind of treasures life had brought his way? The love of a beautiful, caring woman. The gift of a healthy baby girl. Apparently,

Sterling thought precious little of those things, sloughing them off as mere points to be dealt with contractually. The thought of it slayed Blake, angered him.

Surely, Sterling hadn't always been so insensitive and surly. No way someone as sweet and giving as Sam could've fallen in love with him if he had been. Could she?

. . . And could she still be in love with the man?

The question had plagued Blake all afternoon, though he went through the motions of the day as if nothing were wrong. He'd met with a friend of Dom's who needed advice on a property easement contract and picked up another mahogany bookcase for his office. But all the while his thoughts kept going back to Sam . . . wondering how she must feel . . . what she might be thinking . . . what decisions she'd made.

. . . She said she missed me!

Never had words sounded—and felt—so good. So good, that he had to look away quickly and pick up Emma for fear Sam would have seen the genuine pleasure in his eyes. Yet he wondered exactly what her words had meant. Had she missed his help with Emma? Simply missed having another body nearby to talk to? Or had she missed *him?*

. . . The way I miss her?

Ah, well the answers may soon be at hand. He clenched his teeth at the thought. Picking up the car keys from his dresser, he caught a glimpse of his reflection in the mirror, and noticed the unusually stern set of his jaw. And no wonder. Dom had called to say that Sam hoped the four of them could meet at her house around six-thirty—her, Blake, Dom and Maria. Apparently, she needed a chance to talk to them altogether.

I wonder, he thought, closing the door of his condo behind him, *if they'll be words I care to hear.*

Aunt Maria insisted on holding Emma the minute she walked through Sam's front door. It made for a sweet picture, the dark-haired French woman sitting on the couch with the pinkish, pale-haired baby, and a glowing Uncle Dom snuggled up so close to them both that he was practically in her aunt's lap too.

They looked so happy she hated to give them her news. News that was sure to cause them personal concern and make them wonder about Emma's future. But Sam had struggled with the issues all afternoon, and there didn't seem to be any other way.

The doorbell rang, interrupting her thoughts. Her heart skipped a beat knowing it had to be Blake.

Poor Blake. How awful she felt about everything with him too! Why had she ever dragged him into all of this? And now, with the way things were, he might get hurt even more.

She opened the door to him, the pounding of her heart seeming to drown out the sound of her voice. "Hi."

"Hope I'm not too late." He attempted a smile. But for once, Sam noticed, it fell short.

For a moment, she wondered—mostly hoped—that his words held some sort of double meaning. But in reality she knew she had no right to wish such things . . .

"No, you're perfect," she replied, blushing at the involuntary softness in her tone. "Come in."

Uncle Dom sat forward on the couch long enough to heartily shake Blake's hand before the younger man settled into an overstuffed chair adjacent to the sofa.

Sam sat down in the matching chair across from

Blake, her stomach churning. While the three of them chatted on non-stop about Emma, her mind swirled with a jumble of thoughts, her limbs feeling more leaden by the second.

How should she begin to tell them everything? What exactly would the right words be? After all, they were all here now, ready to listen. There was no turning back. And once the words were out of her mouth . . . well, she just hoped they wouldn't be too upset and angry with her.

"Thank you all for coming," she began, squeezing her tense hands in her lap.

How trite! I sound like an emcee at a charity event.

"You're welcome, dear," her aunt answered brightly. "Have you had any dinner yet?"

"Dinner?" The question threw Sam off guard. "Uh, Emma has eaten, but um, no, I really didn't think about—"

"Well, good then." Aunt Maria continued to sway with Emma. "I took the liberty of ordering pizzas. Hope you don't mind."

"Pizzas?" Would anyone be in the mood to eat after she got finished telling them about the decision she'd made today?

Uncle Dom seemed to notice the look of consternation on Sam's face and chimed in. "If that's not alright, we can always order up something else too."

Sam unraveled her hands and waved them in the air. "No, no, pizzas are fine. It's just that, well . . ."

She glanced at Blake who already knew what had transpired today with Prescott's contract and all. Half-expecting him to jump in the way he always did and help her out, she felt a bit disappointed when he didn't.

But then why would he? She reminded herself. She'd already told him to forget about ever being involved. But only because she'd been angry and confused . . . and embarrassed at the time. And now, seeing the reservation in his eyes she wished she'd never said such a thing.

"Spit it out, honey," Uncle Dom urged. "It can't be that bad."

She spoke solemnly. "It might be, Uncle Dom."

"Is there something wrong with the baby?" Fear widened his eyes. Aunt Maria and Blake shot concerned looks at her too.

"No, no. Emma is fine," Sam assured them all with a shake of her head.

Blake piped up. "Dr. Farrell said she's moving into the euphoric, smiling state."

"Oh, pooh. She's just a delightful, happy child, aren't you, Emma?" Maria cooed to the baby.

"I happen to think so, too," Blake readily agreed.

"And her eyes seem to be bluer than they were," her uncle observed. "Is that possible? Did you ask the doctor about that?" He turned to Blake.

Obviously, Sam had lost control of her audience. "Please, everyone!" she blurted out, standing up. "There's something important I have to say, and it could impact all of your lives. So, so—" she rubbed her clammy palms together, "I need to say it."

Her outburst definitely got their attention and silenced the room. In fact, the room was so quiet it almost made it harder to speak.

"Uncle Dom, um . . ." She paused and bit her lip. "You told me recently that I had, uh, a good mind and a caring heart, and to use them both." She could barely look at the three of them as she spoke. "And well, I don't know if you all will think I'm so caring when I say this. But I did something today, and I had to do it. I mean, it was the only way I could follow my heart, like you said." Wringing her hands, she looked at her uncle, then at her aunt and Blake.

"But knowing Genevieve Sterling as well as I do, there could be a backlash. Some awful repercussions. You are all tenants of hers and you never know what that woman will do. And I, well, now that it's just me, I . . ." A sob began to form in the back of her throat. "I mean, I make a pretty decent salary, so I'll do my best to give Emma . . ."

She collapsed back into the chair, tears beginning to trickle onto her cheeks. She was making a mess of this, botching it up completely.

Leaning forward, her uncle laid his hands over hers. "What are you saying, sweetheart?" he asked softly.

"I'm saying . . . what I'm saying is, I'm no longer engaged to Prescott," she replied, unable to face her uncle. "I broke things off with him today. He isn't the right person for me—or for Emma."

With that, her uncle jumped to his feet.

"Haha!" he shouted gleefully. "That's wonderful news, Sam!" He turned swiftly to Blake. "Isn't it, B.D.? What do you think?"

"I'd say, I'd say it's positively sensational." Blake sounded shocked and pleased all at the same time.

"It is?" Sam lifted her head to see three smiling faces in front of her. Make that four, now that Emma had entered her infant euphoric state. All beaming at her like she'd just won a sweepstakes or something.

How could they all be so overjoyed? She wondered. She had broken off her engagement just hours ago. That was a serious thing; she had almost made a grave mistake. The man she thought loved her, the man she had proposed to spend the rest of her life with, wasn't the man she thought he was at all. Her life was completely topsy-turvy now. She had turned away a fiancé and taken in a baby girl.

Granted it was better to discover Prescott's true colors now rather than later. But there was still a certain sadness attached to the turn of affairs. She felt depleted, defeated. Like she'd lost a battle of some kind, like she had failed. And the fact that the three people in her family room were whooping with pleasure made her feel like even more of a failure. Obviously from their reaction they'd known Prescott wasn't right for her all along—something she'd taken months and months to figure out.

Her uncle paused in his jubilation long enough to address her. "Now, Samantha, honey, I don't want you to worry about baby Emma. We all believe you'll make a great mother. If, you know," he stumbled, adding haltingly, "things turn out that way. And if they do, you don't ever have to feel like you're alone. We'll all be nearby to support you, whatever you two girls need."

Her uncle's compassion touched her immensely, bringing tears tingling at the corners of her eyes. But it was the glance from Blake that clutched at her heart. All of his earlier reserve had dissipated from his eyes. Despite the curt words she'd spoken to him this afternoon, his look told her he still cared. "Thank you . . ." she whispered hoarsely, glimpsing at all of them, her gaze falling last on the Englishman.

"Oh, sweetie," her aunt said soothingly as she bounced Emma gently on her lap. "You did the right thing. The best thing. It'll be fine."

"You'll feel better once the pizza gets here." Her uncle patted her on the knee. "I know I will. I'm starving."

Pausing Emma in mid-bounce, Maria looked over her shoulder out the bay window behind the sofa. "I think that's the delivery man now."

"Time to celebrate!" Her uncle clapped his hands together as he made a path to the front door.

"I guess . . . I'll get some plates ready . . . some napkins . . ." Sam said tentatively, still somewhat taken aback that her serious gathering had turned into a pizza party.

"I'll help." Blake followed her into the kitchen.

As always, the two of them seemed to fall into sync with one another. She got the dishes down from the cupboard while he began to fill glasses with ice. But as they each turned to place the plates and glasses on the oak table, they nearly collided.

Deftly, Blake set the glasses on the table and turned to her to release the heavy plates from her hands. At that, their fingers touched and a sudden glow of warmth flashed between them, molding them to the moment.

Looking up, she saw his eyes turn dark and desirous, making her heart quicken in her chest. Causing her lashes to flutter like fans working to cool the burning intensity and caring she saw there.

"Blake, I'm sorry." Her voice cracked contritely. "What I said today. It was so wrong of me. And I didn't really mean—"

"Shh." He placed a finger on her lips with one hand, and took the dishes from her with the other. Setting them on the table, he turned back to her, stepping even closer.

Her breath caught in her chest as he took her hand, pulling her toward him. Gracefully, artfully, as if they were dancing and he was leading their steps, he drew her into the circle of his arms. A place that felt familiar and right—like they'd been partners in this dance of intimacy many times before.

"Don't apologize," he whispered hoarsely. "Sometimes one simply gets caught up in the moment. Don't you think?"

Before she could answer, before she *could* think, he lowered his head. And his lips, his soft lips met hers with a combination of sweetness and passion like she'd never known before.

So this is what it's like to be kissed. To be really kissed.

Her mind reeled. Her limbs tingled at the unexpected pleasure she felt. And just as she was thinking how much she wanted the moment to last, he pulled away from her.

Ever so gently, he brushed a strand of her hair back from her face. His hand kept smoothing the spot at her temple as if he couldn't stop touching her.

"I won't say I'm sorry for that, Sam," his voice sounded low and husky, "because I'm not. But I promise I'll never do it again. Unless, of course," his fingers stopped stroking, but his gaze remained steady, "you want me to."

Chapter Nine

April ducked her head into Sam's office, a worried expression creasing her brow. "Chief McKnight is on the phone."

Generally, April let Sam know about incoming calls via the intercom. But Somersby's chief of police was an exception, a call April announced privately, quietly. The two women had never talked about it, but April seemed to intuitively know the chief's calls rattled Sam. Actually, they seemed to upset April somewhat, too.

During Emma's weeklong stay at the agency, the adorable infant managed to capture the hearts of all Sam's co-workers. In fact, when they heard Sam's aunt offered to provide childcare for Emma throughout the workday, they were thrilled for Sam. But they were noticeably saddened, too. No one wanted to see "baby sunshine" leave the agency.

They even held a going-away baby shower for Emma complete with presents, cake and lots of tears. And every day since it never failed that someone didn't stop by to inquire about Emma's well-being, or ask to see an up-dated photo of her.

So it wasn't surprising that Sam wasn't the only one at the agency holding her breath when the chief called. Who knew what McKnight would have to report? That he had found Emma's parents? Discovered a strong lead? That he was coming to take the precious baby girl away?

Sam tried to appear calm though her heart pounded in her chest at such thoughts. "Thanks, April."

April nodded sympathetically and held up crossed fingers for good luck before backing out the door.

Arm rigid, hand tense, Sam picked up the phone. "Chief McKnight?"

"Sorry to bother you at work again, Miss Stevenson." His voice sounded strong and commanding, resonant as a radio deejay's.

"No bother," she replied politely. It wasn't a bother, but it was bothersome.

For the past month and a half or so, Sam had been going through the same motions every day. Packing up Emma's things in the morning. Dropping the baby off at Aunt Maria's on her way to the agency. Calling to check up on her throughout the day. Running errands at lunch to buy formula, diapers, bottle liners. Picking up Emma after work, enjoying the evening with her—and quite often Blake too. Rocking her to sleep at night. Watching, totally fascinated, as Emma's little chest moved up and down as she slept.

All the while, feeling more and more as if Emma belonged to her. Feeling more and more as if all her actions weren't just a routine, but her new life. A life with Emma that would never, ever end.

But then the chief would call, and interrupt all of that with a dose of reality. Painful reality.

"Just wanted to give you our latest report, ma'am."

Sam closed her eyes and held her breath just as she did every time McKnight spoke those words on the other end of the line. Quickly, she uttered a prayer for "whatever is right for Emma." Then she added her usual tag to the petition, "And please, if You would, Lord, make me the person who's right for her."

Seemingly unaware of the emotional trauma his updates caused, the chief spoke blithely, "It seems we still don't have a credible lead."

A deep exhale exited her body, relief filling all the empty pockets it left behind. A bright sureness lifted her voice. "Really? Well, that's no problem. I mean she's a great baby. I'm happy to care for her. No problem at all."

Thank goodness! she sighed. *Now Thanksgiving will be perfect tomorrow. Emma will still be with us. Surrounded by people we love, people who love her. What a lot to be thankful for!*

Aunt Maria and Uncle Dom were hosting the holiday affair, and Blake would be there, too, of course, along with some other company as well.

Blake's brother Phillip and sister-in-law Cara were flying in from Boston with young Blake, their three-year-old son, late this evening, and planned to stay overnight at the Manor Inn.

And the biggest surprise of all—Sam's parents were coming. Somehow Janie and Thomas Stevenson had managed to set aside their differences for the time being and agreed to fly out from opposite coasts to spend the holiday with their daughter in Somersby.

Well, not to be with *her* really, Sam realized. Obviously, this wasn't normal procedure for the two of them. In the years since their separation, she'd had the stressful task of choosing between her parents, then hopping on a plane to go spend the holiday with one or the other of them.

But not this year. Not since Emma.

Though her parents could be stubborn with one another at times, they were also curious—especially about a prospective granddaughter. Too curious not to take this opportunity to come.

Amazing what power a fifteen pound, two ounce being wields!

Honestly, Sam didn't care what the catalyst was. She couldn't wait for them to meet Emma. Couldn't wait to see her mom and dad together again. The thought of having both parents in the same room, sharing a Thanksgiving feast overwhelmed her with a sweet, nostalgic feeling.

And she was just as anxious to meet some of Blake's family. Would Phillip be anything like his brother Blake? She wondered. As handsome? Caring? And full of surprises?

She glanced at a frame on the corner of her desk. Inside it was darling Emma all dressed up in a pumpkin outfit from Blake. He had appeared on her doorstep the Sunday before Halloween with the outfit, complete with a pumpkin "lid"—a hat that tied under Emma's baby-soft cheeks.

Deemed Emma's first Halloween costume, they had taken at least a dozen pictures of her. Some inside the house surrounded by pumpkins Sam had carved. Others outside on Sam's wraparound porch, the two of them taking turns sitting on the bale of hay with the baby pumpkin in their lap.

She found herself grinning at the memory of that day. Grinning, when she was supposed to be listening to the chief.

". . . so I'd be lying if I didn't tell you that I'm concerned, Miss Stevenson," the chief's imposing voice continued on. What was he talking about? *Concerned? About what?*

Sam shot up in her chair, instantly defensive. "Believe me, Chief McKnight, we care about Emma immensely. We're doing everything right by her, I swear."

"Oh, it's not the baby I'm concerned about, ma'am," he paused before adding more delicately, "It's you."

"Me?"

Sam could almost feel him nod over the phone. "Each day you have that baby is another day you have to become more deeply attached to her."

Become attached? That baby stole my heart the moment I laid eyes on her. A moment. A day. Two months. The amount of time doesn't matter.

"I appreciate the concern, but there's no need to worry about me, Chief."

Everything will work out right. It has to. I was meant to have Emma.

"Ma'am, I don't mean to sound rude, but there's still a good possibility that we'll locate the parents. I just don't want you to lose sight of that," he said sincerely. "Can't forget that, you know?"

"Sure. Of course. I understand," she said, agreeing in theory, but not in her heart.

* * *

As Sam opened her front door, Blake stood there loosening his navy-striped tie, unbuttoning the top button of his pale blue shirt tucked under his wool topcoat. With his briefcase hanging heavily from his other hand and the winter sky darkening behind him, he looked every bit the weary provider home from a day of knocking heads with the world.

Actually, she probably appeared much the same to him, she realized. Standing there in her stockinged feet, holding Emma over her left shoulder, she looked every bit as frazzled. Her gray slacks were rumpled from the day, her hair disheveled, and she could feel Emma's drool seeping through the back of her untucked turtleneck.

Still, he gazed at her with such intense warmth, she felt as if she looked like perfection, as if his one look at her could make all the concerns of his day melt away.

"Hey." His lopsided grin surfaced.

"Hi," she responded breathlessly, an explosive spontaneous smile lighting up her face the way it always did when she saw him.

The moment had all the right props for a coming home scene between a young couple reuniting at the workday's end. Everything . . .

. . . but the kiss.

His kiss.

Sam had thought about it dozens of times, recalling that night in her kitchen when he had taken her in his arms and kissed her. Really kissed her in a way she'd never experienced before. Though it had been nearly a month, she hadn't gone a day without reliving the feel of his lips . . . or recalling the dark longing in his eyes.

The memory always left her yearning for the day it would happen again.

But, as Blake had made clear—had actually promised—he wouldn't allow it to happen again. And unfortunately—at least in this situation—he was a man of his word. He'd never approached her after that. Not in that way, anyway. If their relationship were to take a more serious turn, she knew the next move had to be hers when the time was right. Yet with every passing day, she wondered if the time would ever be right.

"Come on in," she said.

She stepped back, letting his presence fill her home. Wondering if she would ever take the initiative to have him fill her heart.

Soon after she'd parted ways with Prescott—well, "parting ways" was putting it mildly. In reality, once she'd simmered down about the addendum to the prenup, she'd paid a visit to Prescott's office. She had hoped to talk things over and return the engagement ring in a delicate, sensitive way. But evidently, Prescott wasn't in a talking mood. He'd practically had security throw her out of his building.

Anyway, at that time it seemed fickle and even a bit inappropriate to be kissing another man so soon. So she had waited. Waited for some designated appropriate moment. But that specific time remained elusive. In fact, it never seemed to come. And as time moved on, her feelings for Blake became stronger and more certain. Yet—her nerve seemed just the opposite, growing more timid and unsure.

What if, after all those weeks, Blake had changed his mind? What if he didn't feel quite the same way as he had before?

Sure, they spent almost every evening and weekend afternoons together, but it was always with Emma. Always the three of them. No doubt he cared for Emma. He doted on her as if she were his own. But what about her? What feelings did he hold for her?

If he really, really cared for her, felt passionate about her, how could he possibly contain himself? And yet . . . sometimes the way he looked at her . . .

Well, it was enough to make a girl wonder, she thought as she watched him hoist his briefcase onto her antique bench, snap it open, take something out and close it back again.

He turned to face her, holding out a medium-sized cayenne-colored gift bag.

"What is it?" She blinked.

"A surprise." He grinned. He removed his overcoat and suit coat in a single motion, tossed them on the bench, too, then held out his arms . . . for Emma.

"A surprise, huh?" She handed the infant over, smiling up at him teasingly. "Not a turkey outfit for Emma to wear tomorrow, is it?"

"Are you still poking fun at the pumpkin costume I bought for Em?" He adjusted the infant, making a cradle for her in his strong, welcoming arms. "Because I happen to know you loved it. And, you, Princess," he bent over to whisper in Emma's ear, "looked adorable in it, I might add."

"I did love it. I just didn't know if you'd be bringing by some sort of Thanksgiving costume, too," she taunted.

"What? Something along the lines of a festive fowl?" He grimaced. "I think not. Do I look like the sort of man who would have you dress Emma like poultry? I have much better taste than that, don't I, little bugaboo?" He lowered his head to rub noses with Emma, Eskimo-style.

The fun-loving gesture evoked a gurgling laugh from the baby, bringing on more silly gibberish from him. "Bugaboo. Bugaboo. Bugaboo," he chanted, rubbing his head at Emma's tummy, eliciting more delightful sounds from her.

Meanwhile Sam looked on smiling, totally captivated. How irresistibly charming he looked—and silly, too! A six-foot virile male being reduced to nonsensical babble by a tiny, baby girl.

"And actually," Blake added, when he came up for air, "the package isn't for Emma anyway. It's for you."

"For me? Blake, you don't have to bring presents."

A lock of hair had fallen onto his forehead, making him look endearingly boyish.

You're more than enough, she wanted to say. *Just you being here, your laughter, your presence, fills this house like it's never been filled.*

"Well, you're always going to the trouble of cooking." He shrugged, then lifting Emma to his shoulder, rubbed her small back soothingly.

"Not always. You brought over that pasta dish from Brio's last night. And the Thai food on Sunday. Besides, I'm just making a little meatloaf."

"And this is only a little present." He grinned. "Don't make such an issue of it. It's not that impressive, believe me." He continued patting the baby. "Nothing like a three-carat diamond ring anyway."

The comment froze them both, making the room feel unbearably silent. It was a moment before Blake shook his head, seeming to be disgusted with himself.

"I didn't mean that the way it sounded."

"I'm sure you didn't," she said sincerely. No doubt he wouldn't want to remind her of her former fiancé and the ring she'd returned to Prescott the month before.

"What I meant to say is, it's just something a client of mine crafted."

Something handmade.

Besides the showy engagement ring, Prescott had only given her one other gift in the years they were together. A diamond encrusted watch, which as it turned out, wasn't a token of his love, but rather a jibe at her. An expensive request that she try harder to adapt her schedule so she could be on time for Genevieve's events and dinners.

"May I?" She nodded at the bag in her hand, anxious to see the handcrafted gift the Englishman had picked out just for her.

He nodded, a hint of shyness in his expression. "Certainly."

Though she had teased about a holiday outfit for Emma, she knew all along from the weight and size of the bag that it was far too bulky for that. Peeking inside, she saw a blend of colors that delighted her eyes. Mulberry, chartreuse, rust, taupe.

"Oh, Blake, it's beautiful!" She took a striped scarf from the bag, holding the cuddly knitted wool up to her cheeks. "And so soft."

"There's a hat in there, too," he told her, still patting Emma's back. "I have a client who had them both on display in her store. You probably know her. The owner of the Lambikins Knit Shop? Nancy Dunaway?"

"She's married to a friend of mine."

"Anyway, as I said, the set was on display—and not

at all for sale. But . . ." He tilted his head, smiling drolly. Probably, he would've shrugged his shoulders smugly, too, if Emma hadn't been resting there.

"But you talked her into selling it with that irresistible British accent of yours, right?"

His eyes glittered at her words. "I didn't know you found my accent irresistible."

A flush rushed to her cheeks. "Well, I didn't mean *me* exactly," she stammered. "But, you know, most women, they, uh, kind of fall for that sort of thing."

Why was she so nervous suddenly? So serious? Why couldn't she be light and flirtatious right back at him? Why didn't she tell him honestly—*I love your accent, I love the hours we spend together, I love the way you kissed me . . .*

"Then I suppose Mrs. Dunaway is most women. Good thing, too. The scarf and hat go too perfectly with those gloves of yours."

"My gloves?"

"The chartreuse ones. You had them on the first day I met you. In Chausseures'."

He remembered her gloves? The details of the day they first met?

Suddenly, the time seemed more right than ever to kiss him. She wanted so desperately to thank him for being the sweetest man she'd ever known. To show him how she really felt. Shyly, she took a step forward. But then she wondered what he'd think of her, and her legs locked. They wouldn't move any closer; she was frozen to the spot.

"You're right, they'll go perfectly. Thank you so much."

"You're quite welcome."

If he was disappointed his gift didn't evoke so much as a thank-you kiss on the cheek, he didn't let it show. Unfettered, he started for the kitchen. "Has Baby Em had her bottle yet?"

"You can feed her while I put dinner on the table if you'd like." Her steps trailed after him.

With Emma still on his shoulder, Blake expertly prepared the baby's bottle one-handed, using Sam's arm to test the temperature of the formula. Then he settled contently into a kitchen chair, feeding Emma while Sam worked around the two of them, setting the table and finishing up supper.

"You seem to be getting a lot of clients lately."

"A slew of small business owners." He nodded. "Quite a diversion from the major corporations I represented in Boston. Actually," he looked up from feeding Emma, "it has me thinking."

"Thinking? About what?"

"Well, I'm realizing that small businesses require quite a bit of savvy to survive. For instance, Nancy Dunaway knows all there is to know about knitting and yarn. But as a business owner, she also needs to know about leases, legal matters, payroll, taxes, inventory, and so on."

"Wow," she replied, spacing silverware and napkins on a pair of paisley cloth placemats, "I never thought about it like that."

"I'm thinking perhaps I could offer small business owners all those services in one package so they could then concentrate solely on the nature of their business."

"Can you do that?" She moved back to the stove, stirring a pot of simmering green beans. "I mean, cover all of those areas?"

"Not on my own." He set Emma's half-empty bottle

on the table. Hugging her to his shoulder, he patted her back attempting to elicit a burp. "But I may be able to get my youngest brother Drew to move here. He's a whiz at accounting, computers. That sort of thing."

"Oh!" She turned excitedly, pointing a wooden spoon in his direction. "April has a girlfriend who recently opened a café on the east side. Smart woman. Ambitious. Really cute, too. It sounds like she could use some outside help, especially some accounting expertise like your brother has."

"Trying to play matchmaker for the Dawson clan, are you?"

"Me? Of course not." She waved the spoon sternly in the air. "Strictly business, I swear." But she couldn't restrain the playful smile that broke out on her face.

"Uh, huh. That's what all you females say."

With that, Emma gave a loud, hearty burp, making the two adults giggle. It reminded Sam of one of those first nights when she'd been alone with Emma . . . the night she realized how much she missed Blake's presence, how much she enjoyed being with him.

She started to tell him about it. Tell him all about how she felt that night, what her feelings were for him now. Maybe then, after that, it would be the right time to move toward him, to kiss him. But instead she said, "Chief McKnight called today."

Blake's hand stopped patting instantly. His mouth dropped open, starting to form a question. But none came. Raised eyebrows did the asking for him.

She shook her head in response. "Nothing to report."

A long sigh escaped from him, and Sam watched as he lovingly caressed Emma's tiny torso. Lightly kissing the crown of the wispy-haired head tucked underneath his chin, he closed his eyes momentarily. Laying his dark-haired head against Emma's fair one, he seemed to be taking a moment of quiet thanks. Then he turned the baby girl around in his arms, letting Em nurse the remainder of the bottle.

"Are you anxious to see your mum and pop tomorrow?" he asked quietly, reflectively.

The words barely registered on Sam at first, she was so caught up in Blake's touching display of emotion. She wasn't the only one deeply affected by Emma's presence in her life, was she? The strain, the relief, it had all been apparent in his face and reaction.

"I really am," she told him, suddenly feeling closer to him than ever before. "It's been years since the three of us have been in the same room together. Actually," she paused, recalling the awful night several years before, "I think the last time that happened is when I got the news they were separating."

"Ouch!" He clenched his teeth.

She nodded glumly. "No kidding."

Dinner was nearly ready, but Emma still had a couple of ounces to go. Turning down the burners on the stove, Sam sat down in the chair across from Blake. Emma's sucking noises sounded oddly comforting.

"Probably not an easy thing at any age, I suppose."

"Honestly, I would've thought being in my twenties and on my own, I would've handled it better." She sighed in remembrance. "But that wasn't the reality. I was angry. Confused. And felt awfully betrayed."

She noticed Blake kept his focus on Emma when he asked, "Is that about the same time you met Sterling?"

"Close to that time, I suppose. But by then my feelings had changed again. When he asked me to marry him—

well, I'm almost too embarrassed to say . . ." She rolled her eyes at her own foolishness. "But I wrote it all down on paper, a pros and cons list, just like I used at my work or when deciding to buy a new car or something. Can you imagine?"

Confounded and chagrined by her admission, she lowered her gaze from his. Her hand worked to smooth out a wrinkle in the placement, as if that would set the world right.

"It's okay," his voice soothed, caressing her as if he had a free hand to reach out and touch her. The caring, non-judgmental look in his eyes told her he meant it. "On paper, I would assume Sterling looked pretty good," he offered with a half-grin.

"Plus," she nodded, "by that time I'd gotten over my initial feelings about the separation. And by then I was just so, so—"

"Numb?"

"Totally. After the anger, the disappointment, I couldn't feel a thing."

"But that's not how you seem now."

"It's not how I feel now."

You came along, and everything changed from that day on.

Her mouth wanted to form the words, but instead her hands were busy straightening the silverware on the placemat, making the utensils line up perfectly, squarely. Hesitating . . . stalling.

What are you waiting for? She scolded herself. *Say it!*

But instead . . .

"Emma came into my life, and everything changed from that day on."

"Maybe Emma will change your parents' lives, too."

He paused long enough to remove the empty bottle from Emma's pursed lips. "Seems she already has them reuniting in a neutral part of the country."

"A little ambassador of love, huh?" she said wistfully.

They both stared fondly at the precious gift they were lucky to share, and chuckled at the dear sight of her working to keep her droopy eyelids open.

Blake whispered softly, "How about a lullaby, Little One?"

Not cognizant of his words, but apparently moved the by the familiar sweet tone of his voice, Emma offered him a sleepy smile. Cuddling her wee body in the safety of his muscular arms, he carried her into the spare bedroom.

When Emma first arrived, her crib with its lamb-covered bedding took up only a corner of the extra room. But little by little Sam and Maria couldn't resist redecorating. Adding an antique rocker, a teddy bear lamp, a changing table topped with stuffed animals, and large wooden blocks that spelled out Emma's name, the room was transformed into the baby's own.

As Sam served their dinner onto plates, Blake's attempts at a lullaby drifted in from Emma's room, making her grin. For all the ways the Englishman was incredibly attractive, his singing did not make the list. Still, his clipped phrasing and off-key notes never hindered Emma from falling asleep in no time.

By the time they finished eating dinner and cleaning up dishes it was late, nearly time for Blake to head for the airport to meet Phillip's and Cara's plane. He wanted to be on time, figuring little Blake would be exhausted.

As Sam walked him to her front door to say goodnight, it crossed her mind that each night it was growing harder and harder to part from him. They seemed to linger there on her threshold, looking for even the most banal thing to say—anything so their time together didn't have to come to an end.

"You're very sure you want to challenge me?" he asked her, referring to their Thanksgiving pie bake-off. "You can still get out of it, you know. Last chance." He picked up his coat from the bench, pulling it over his broad shoulders.

"What? Just each bring a pie to Uncle Dom's and Aunt Maria's? Not wager bets on them? You must be getting nervous about your baking skills. Scared off after my triple berry cobbler tonight?"

"The cobbler *was* fairly delicious, I suppose." He cocked his head thoughtfully. "For your first attempt anyway."

"Fairly delicious? That's why you had two helpings, I guess?"

He laughed. "I hated for you to have all that left over."

"Oh, you are *so* sweet," she replied facetiously, elongating the words.

He inclined his head toward hers, replying huskily, "Much sweeter than you know." Then straightening, he added with a shrug "So sweet, I don't want you to feel sorely tomorrow when everyone chooses my pie over yours."

"And smug too." She grinned. "Typical Englishman, huh?" Then picking up the scarf from the bench in the entryway, she added, "True, you have good taste in clothing, but I'm not worried about your baking abilities. I think my pumpkin pie will beat yours."

Before she knew what had happened, with a whisk of his hand he slipped the scarf out of her grasp and twirled it around her head. It landed around her neck, the soft-ness feeling deliciously cozy against her skin. Then he grabbed each end of the scarf and drew her near to him.

His eyes gleamed with playfulness, and his lips, so close, seemed to tug at hers with a magical attraction. Instantly, memories of their first kiss flooded her being, quickened her heart, nearly stopped her breath. She stood still, gaping, waiting in sweet anticipation for her second chance with him.

Then ever so gently with his fingertip he traced the line of her nose, dabbing it at the end for good measure.

"Better get baking then." He smiled into her eyes.

Chapter Ten

"**I** wish I could think of something more profound to say. But at the moment, the thing I'm most thankful for is the chance to eat this delicious-looking meal in peace!"

All the adults sitting around the Thanksgiving table laughed at Cara's comment. And no one could blame the young mother for it. Three-year-old Blake, as adorable as he was, had kept her on her toes since the minute they walked into Aunt Maria and Uncle Dom's house.

First, he had raced through the ranch-style house, arms spread wide, mimicking the jet their family had flown on the night before. Then he became intrigued with baby Emma, trying to poke at her, feed her trail mix from a candy dish on the table, and once Sam laid Emma in the safety of her porta-pen, he had even tried to climb in and join her.

But both Cara and Phillip maintained a great sense of humor where his "zest for living" was concerned. Sam took a liking to the couple instantly.

"I tell you," Phillip had addressed the table earlier in his distinguished British way, "I can hold the attention of a boardroom full of trustees any day of the week. But my three-year-old son? I practically have to stand on my head to get him to listen to me."

Luckily, for his parents' sake, the younger Blake wore himself out just about the time dinner was served. Glancing across her aunt and uncle's dining room into the family room, Sam could see the small tyke fast asleep on Maria's floral couch, a cream-colored afghan pulled up to his chin.

She also had a good view of Emma, too, snuggled under her yellow lamb-printed quilt in the porta-pen. Though she had thought Emma would be too agitated to nap after being passed around and held by everyone, the baby had settled down easily after her bottle.

As silverware clinked and quiet chatting and laughter ensued, Sam wondered at how different a house seemed when little ones inhabited it. Awake and even asleep, they filled up a home with an intangible aura that felt singularly special and blessed.

"Is it getting warm in here?" Blake turned to her, interrupting her thoughts.

"Pardon me?"

"You're as cherry red as your sweater," he smiled. "I thought you might be getting warm. Or," he winked roguishly and whispered, "perhaps it's the fact that you're sitting next to me that has given you such a glow."

It *was* him, she admitted to herself. She'd watched in awe as he'd won over her parents in the first moments they'd been introduced, no easy task especially where her mother was concerned. Janie Stevenson could be snobbish at times, and had been less than thrilled about losing a future millionaire son-in-law. But the more Blake talked, the more her mother's eyes sparkled, and Sam knew he'd managed to charm her too.

It was also her parents too. They seemed so civil with one another, the way they used to be years before the separation. And the beaming smiles on their faces when they held Emma was like nothing Sam had ever witnessed.

And then Blake's brother and his family. What a pleasure to meet them! She wished they lived down the street from her. And Aunt Maria and Uncle Dom, they were always there for her no matter what.

And Emma . . . what a joy. Her heart welled up with emotion. She bit the inside of her cheeks trying to stop her eyes from spilling over with tears.

"I'm—I'm just thankful everyone's here," she whispered hoarsely to him. "Together," her voice cracked.

Reaching under the tablecloth, Blake found her hand on her lap and squeezed it gently. His eyes caressed hers knowingly.

"What did you say, honey?" Uncle Dom's antennas had suddenly tuned her in. "What are you thankful for?"

Throughout dinner, their banter had been interspersed with each person's reason for thanks. Maria had led off by saying she was thankful for the bountiful blessing of their meal. Dom had chimed in jocularly saying he was grateful it'd be Sam's turn to play Thanksgiving host the following year.

Wedged in a chair between Dom and Cara, Phillip had spoken up next, giving a heartwarming speech of gratitude to his brother for times past, namely, for the year

Blake spent in Germany for Phillip. And for times present, inviting Phillip's family to share the holiday.

Blake, though visibly moved, sloughed off the sentimentality. "You're my older brother. I had to do those things. You'd have pounded me otherwise." Everyone laughed, and Cara then further lightened the mood with her quip about eating in peace.

And now her uncle was asking her what she was grateful for, and she was too overwhelmed to speak. However, Blake, gallant man that he always was, came to her rescue.

"I'll tell you what I'm thankful for," he interjected, giving Sam a momentary reprieve. "I'm very thankful for towns such as Somersby, Ohio. Somersby, and the people in it, of course." He raised his glass in salute, and everyone followed in kind.

Sam knew he'd intentionally diverted everyone's attention to give her a chance to get her gush of feelings under control. Swallowing her emotions, she was just about to speak up when her father completely passed her over.

"I'll tell you what. I'll be grateful when the Buffalo Bills win today," he said huskily to the other men at the table. "I've got a couple hundred bucks on them."

"No kidding?" Dom looked up from his plate. "I've got fifty riding on them."

Men! A chuckle started to form in the back of Sam's throat.

"Dad, it's supposed to be something you're thankful for. Something a little more serious than football."

Phillip cocked an eyebrow in mock sternness. "Football is the ultimate in seriousness, Samantha."

Blake piped up. "Especially when you're betting on the Bills."

"What? You don't think they can win?" Her father almost barked the question. "Their new quarterback did great last week."

"Well, that's true." Blake considered. "I don't know. I hope for your sake, both of your sakes," he included Dom, "they rally and pull this one off."

Sam suddenly noticed her mother poking at her food, looking thoughtfully down at her plate. "Mom, are you okay?" she asked softly. "You look like you're thinking about something other than sports."

Her mother looked up, tilting her head at Sam. "I've forgotten how good it feels to hold a little one in my arms again. So hopeful. It's been a long time since I've felt that." She reached across the chair where her somewhat estranged husband sat and touched Sam's arm. "Thank you for that."

Sam patted her mother's hand back. "Thanks for coming. Both of you." She smiled at her parents.

Glossing over the touching moment in his typical way, Uncle Dom turned to his wife, "Maria, darling, that was delicious. Your best turkey ever."

"Incredibly succulent." Blake complimented.

"Incomparably tasty," Phillip seconded.

All the women around the table tittered at the same time, charmed by the accents.

"Anyone ready for dessert?" her uncle glimpsed at everyone.

Cara and Sam groaned simultaneously at the suggestion, rubbing at their tummies.

"B.D., what's this business about a bake-off between you and Samantha?" Dom asked.

"A bake-off?" Phillip scooted back in his chair. "Is that why you asked me to bring one of mum's pumpkin pies along?" He stared at Blake.

Blake cringed. "You'd have never made it in the CIA or Secret Service, Phillip," he said, hunching his shoulders preparing for Sam's verbal assault.

But Janie's voice rang out first. "Oh, I peeked in Samantha's pie dish. It looks like she brought a pumpkin pie from Bonbonnerie Bakery. They are truly wonderful."

"Mo-om," Sam warned in a tone her mother appeared oblivious to.

"What?" Janie shrugged innocently. "I could tell by the signature crust. I don't know why you're making that face, honey. Everything from Bonbonnerie's is delicious."

Blake perked up, facing Sam. "Well, I suppose you've defaulted then."

"Me?"

"You didn't bake a homemade pie. That was our deal, correct?"

Sam cleared her throat, leveling her gaze at him.

"Okay, okay. I see your point. Next year then." He seemed totally sure of himself. "I'll take you on next year. But you'd better be prepared for pie a la Blake."

By the time they'd worked that out, most everyone had already pushed back their chairs from the table. The men started milling around, working their way downstairs to view the football game on the big screen TV. The women began clearing dishes and serving bowls.

Meanwhile, both Sam and Blake heard Emma stirring from the other room. They looked at one another, determining who would go to her. But Blake came up with the best idea yet.

"Janie, would you like to get Emma, and I'll help Sam and Cara clear the table?"

Sam's mom set a stack of bread plates back on the table in a millisecond. "I'd love to." She beamed, scurrying into the living room.

"That was thoughtful of you," Sam told him as they loaded dishes in their arms. "I think you just made a fan for life."

He paused in mid-step, gazing at her intently. "Nothing would please me more."

His words made her cheeks tingle and she wondered, did he really mean the things he said? Did he even realize he said them? Or was it a by-product of his English charm?

Be ready for a bake-off next year? A fan for life— nothing would please him more?

Blushing at the long-term implications, she glanced away from him. As she did, a glimpse of images in the next room caught her attention.

Nudging Blake, she nodded toward the living room. "Look!"

While Janie sat in an overstuffed chair with Emma on her lap, Thomas sat on the arm of the chair, looking down at both of them, a bemused grin on his face. He must have felt Sam and Blake staring at him because he looked up just then.

"Do you have a stroller here?" he asked his daughter.

"A stroller?"

"Your mom and I would like to take Emma for a walk. It's unseasonably warm out there today."

Sam squinted, confused. "Isn't the big game coming on in a minute?"

Her father shrugged nonchalantly, waving his hand. "Ach, nothing happens till after half-time anyway. Besides, I can always catch the highlights later."

As Blake went to fetch the stroller out of the closet, Sam helped her mom snuggle Emma into her one-piece woolen zip-up. Then she and Blake stood at the front door, watching curiously as Janie and Thomas sauntered down the walk with Emma.

"Like you said, a little ambassador of love." Hands in his pockets, Blake rolled back on his heels.

Sam sighed wistfully wishing everything about this wonderful day would never have to end.

Chapter Eleven

"Do you think Em'll tip over in her carrier?" Sam looked up at him, shading her eyes from the glaring sun-snow combination with her gloved hand.

Blake answered her with the sound of his laughter, echoing over the white rolling mounds of the deserted golf course. "Luv, it's the fifth hole on the Camargo Hills Golf Course, not the Grand Tetons. A twenty-five degree incline at best."

He wrapped the light blue and white woolen scarf more tightly around his neck, a leftover souvenir from his days at Columbia. Dressed down in a gray hooded sweatshirt under a brown corduroy car coat, and a pair of faded denims, he had that thrown together, casual look that came off as classically stylish. Effortlessly handsome.

"Besides, I'm at the top of this miniature rise, and you're ten feet away at the bottom. What could possibly happen to her?"

Removing one of his leather gloves, he crouched

down next to Emma's baby carrier and tucked the blanket more snuggly around her. Ten days ago, on Thanksgiving, the weather had been unexpectedly warm. But yesterday the temperature had plunged and by early evening snowflakes began dotting the ebony skies. By sunrise, they had awakened to a glorious crisp-white world, blanketed with at least four inches of snow. That was the fickle weather of the Midwest for you, seasons seeming to change within seasons.

"She could spill out of it and get snow in her face."

"Snow in her face?" He chuckled, replacing his glove. "My dear, you have her wrapped up like a mummy. The only thing showing is her eyes."

"Well, still . . ." She rubbed her hands together briskly, trying to warm them. "Do you think she's cold at all?"

Somewhat exasperated, Blake shook his head at her. "You know, way back in the day you used to be a lot more fun and carefree."

"I did?"

He nodded. "Sure. You took things in stride. Weren't always worried. Much more in control. Yes, indeed, before Emma, everyone wanted to socialize with you because you were so utterly delightful to be with."

"Well, I . . ." She squinted up at him. "Hey, wait a minute, you didn't even know me before Emma."

"See now." He clapped his hands. "There's the joke. And you're so caught up with worry you nearly missed it." He grinned. "Relax, woman," he said easily. "Let's allow this poor child to do a bit of sledding before the sun goes down and all the snow melts away."

"That'll be days from now," she countered.

"True," he smiled tightly, his voice terse, "and it'll soon be days from now if we keep discussing this." He squatted down again by Emma's side. "Okay, are you ready now?" he called down to her. "Because here comes Princess Emma, headed your way."

With that, he gave the plastic bucket carrier the slightest push, starting off Emma's ride. Sam stood below with outstretched arms, waiting to catch her.

For all her worry, Sam had to laugh at the sight of baby and carrier sliding down the slight rise of snow-covered fairway at an almost standstill speed.

"Did she like it?" Blake called from the top, pure glee illuminating his eyes.

"I have no clue." Sam giggled back. "You're right. She's so covered up with a hat, scarves, blankets. All I can see is the white of her eyes."

Picking up the carrier, she gave Emma an impetuous kiss on her cloth-covered nose. "How was that? Hmm, honey? Did you like it? That was your very first sled ride. Well—baby carrier ride."

Crunching through the snow, she carried Emma and her makeshift sled up the rise, meeting Blake halfway on the hill. He smiled at her so brightly, it could've melted the snow. She knew her smile stretched to the limits too. Together, they unwittingly beamed at one another effusively, as if they'd just successfully launched a private spaceship into galaxies unknown.

"Ready for a second try?" His hands covered hers on the handle of the carrier, his eyes glittering with enthusiasm.

A second try? He may have been talking about Emma's sledding. But a second try—a second chance with him—is just what she'd been wishing for.

The sure possessiveness in his hands wrapped around hers felt so familiar. Desirable. And, in the chill of the snow-pure morning, just the two—well, three of them—alone in a hushed white world, the time suddenly seemed more right than ever.

Gathering every bit of nerve she possessed, she grasped the handle more tightly, and leaned over Emma's carrier. Her head turned upwards, timidly she sought his lips with hers. Hungrily, his mouth instinctively greeted hers.

It was so much more of a kiss than the first one they'd shared because they meant so much more to one another now. All their intimate, shared moments . . . all the enjoyable laughter-filled hours . . . even some of the problem-filled days seemed to culminate in the passion and pleasure of that kiss.

"Wow," he said as they broke apart, his voice quiet, as serene as the snow. "Was it something I said?"

"It's everything you've said," she confessed.

Suddenly she felt unusually brave, brazen even. So overwhelmed with her feelings for him, she couldn't fret about the consequences any longer. She simply wanted to let it all out, air her true feelings. Finally. It felt freeing, wonderful. "Everything you've done." Her eyes twinkled fondly. "Everything about you."

"Really, now?" He cocked his head jauntily, looking quite taken with himself. "And . . . would you, uh . . ." He hesitated. "Would you perhaps consider possibly trying that again? That little scenario we just experienced? Like later tonight? When the baby's asleep and we're warm and cozy in front of the fire?"

"Gosh. I don't think so." She smirked, feeling deliciously happy, playful, flirtatious.

He straightened. "What?"

"I don't have a fireplace."

"Oh, yes. Right, right." He gazed at her in wonder. "Sans fire then?" His leather-covered fingers squeezed her gloved hands tenderly.

"Hmm . . . I'll consider it," she teased.

Slipping her hands out from under his, she flipped back the hair hanging under her ski cap.

His eyes narrowed. Giving her a skeptical but amused half-grin he asked, "Is that more of a consider it 'yes' or consider it 'no?' "

"You know," she mocked his British accent, "we really should get the sledding underway. Before the sun goes down and the snow melts away."

"But that will be days from now," he mocked back.

"Yes, and it will be days from now if we stand here and keep discussing this."

Although, in her heart, her light and giddy heart, there was nothing she wanted to do more.

He raised a brow questioningly. "Should I be looking forward to this evening then?"

"I know I will be."

His face registered relief.

"All right. Places everyone," he shouted authoritatively. "More sledding coming right up." Then looking down at a swaddled Emma, "You're with me, darling girl."

They parted ways, him walking uphill, Sam ambling down. As they did, she heard him chattering to the baby. "How did I get to be so lucky, huh? I'm the luckiest man in the . . ."

She didn't hear the rest of the sentence, just enough to make her smile. Just enough to make her feel like the luckiest woman.

* * *

Blake smiled to himself. The candles in the pair of pewter holders on Sam's dining room table didn't look like they'd ever been lit.

Never been used for a romantic dinner, eh?

The thought pleased him as he went about moving them to the low mahogany coffee table in her family room, setting them between the placemats and plates he already placed there alongside the cartons of Chinese carryout.

For a moment, he wondered if Sam might mind him lighting the new-looking candles. He thought about asking, calling back to Emma's room where she was putting the baby down for the night. But then he dismissed the idea instantly. He'd rather surprise her, see her face light up with what he hoped she'd think was an amorous setting.

Besides, if she did mind, he'd simply buy her more tapers, dozens of them if she wished.

As he lit the candles and they glimmered to life, he found himself making a wish that this night would be everything he wanted it to be. For over a month, he'd held himself back from Sam, keeping his word as he'd promised.

It had proved to be the longest month of his life.

So many times, he had squeezed her hand thoughtfully when he'd really wanted to crush her to him passionately, comfort her in his arms. He'd greeted her at the door with a weak smile when a kiss would've said "hello" the way he really wanted to.

And then finally, today, on a deserted snowy golf course no less, she had kissed him. Told him she cared.

I suppose the best things in life really are worth waiting for. He grinned to himself.

A slight vanilla scent from the candles wafted through the air as he put a soft bluesy CD into the player. He turned off two of the three lamps in the room, and tossed a couple of decorative throw pillows on the floor in front of the coffee table.

It may not be the Celestial restaurant or the La-Normandie, but it was the best he could do on short notice. The mood was definitely set.

Hopefully, after their quiet intimate dinner, he'd hold her and tell her all the things he'd kept bottled up inside him for the last month. He'd be playful with her, he thought wistfully. Take in the fresh melon scent of her hair. And . . .

"I can't seem to get her to settle down." Sam trotted back into the room carrying a fussing Emma in her arms. "I don't know if it's her ears, or tummy or what. Something seems to be bothering her."

His spirits dampened somewhat. But his resolve stood firm. This evening was going to be something special.

"Here, let me have a go at it." He held out his hands.

Sam dropped Emma in his arms, then headed straight for the shimmering coffee table.

"Oh, Blake, this looks wonderful," she gushed, openly mesmerized. "Thank you for going to get the food. And you went all the way to Johnny Chan's? Didn't settle for Wong's Express Carry-Out? What a sweetheart you are!"

"Wasn't that major of a deal." He shrugged humbly, rocking the crying Emma steadily.

"And the candles!" Her wide eyes proved her delight.

"You don't mind then?"

"Mind? It's so cozy. And romantic."

Did you hear that, Princess? Blake looked down at Emma. *She thinks it's romantic. So help me out here.*

*Please, little one? I love you dearly, it's true. But I'd
also love to be wooing the other female in my life. What
do you say? Time for beddy bye?*

But all Emma had to say was, "Wahh." Staring up at
him, she continued to whine and fret. Meanwhile, he
continued rocking and walking while Sam peeked into
one of the carryout boxes.

"You got General Tao's chicken! It's my favorite.
Mind if I take a bite?" she asked politely, though she
was already settling onto one of the cushions with fork
in hand. "I'm starving!"

"No, no, not at all," he answered, his heart sinking.

This isn't exactly what I had planned, he thought, pacing the room with the whimpering Emma. *A romantic
dinner for two—eaten one at a time?*

"I got chicken and cashews, too," he found himself
offering.

"You're kidding!" She began opening the remaining
boxes. "That's my other favorite. I swear," she said almost to herself, forking white rice and chicken with
cashews onto her plate, "it's uncanny how you know
these things . . ."

"Yes . . ." he began, his voice lacking any true con-
viction, "I certainly know all about—"

Sam held up her fork-free hand. "Women," she finished the sentence for him as she dug into the food. "You
don't have to convince me."

But what he didn't know all about was—
Baby girls!

He gazed at Emma, his heart turning sympathetic.
"Poor thing."

How can I be the least bit upset with you, precious?

You look so miserable. Teary. Tiny fists clenched. Distraught. Drooling—"

Drooling! He stopped pacing, the wheels in his brain suddenly churning.

Sam looked up, misinterpreting his startled expression. "Don't worry," she said between bites, "I'm saving some for you, too. I'll be done in just a minute. Then I'll take Em and you can eat."

"It's not that," he told her. "I'm just thinking . . . perhaps her teeth are bothering her. Well, her gums actually."

"Oh. I'll bet you're right. I remember reading that. The discomfort can start about any time, can't it? Even if you don't see any teeth erupting?"

He nodded. "Do you have some infant Tylenol?"

"Coming right up." She started to get up.

"No, no, don't interrupt your dinner. Just tell me where it is. I'll get it."

"Don't be silly." She hopped up from the floor. "Besides, I've already finished eating."

Standing next to him, she reached out her arms for Emma. "Why don't you let me give her the Tylenol? You go ahead and eat. It was wonderful, Blake. A great surprise."

He may not have had the chance to share a candlelight dinner with her. But the sweet look she gave him, the warm appreciation in her voice, were intimate and rewarding in another kind of way.

"I'm glad you liked it." He handed the baby to her.

While Sam and Emma went in pursuit of Tylenol, he took a few minutes to eat. It really was delicious, though it would've been even better shared with her.

Like most things . . .

He could hear the two of them in Emma's room, the quiet hushed sounds of the nighttime ritual . . . the creak of the rocker, the muted lullaby coming from the wind-up teddy bear. Finally, as things grew more silenced, he got up and went to stand in the bedroom doorway.

Soothed at last, Em's limp body lay sprawled in Sam's arms. He watched as Sam kissed the baby's forehead and placed her in the crib. Then she came to stand next to him under the threshold.

He wasn't sure whose hand reached for whose first, but suddenly they were standing there, hands clasped tightly together. A warm feeling spread through him, and his heart swelled with something he couldn't quite articulate.

"It's unreal, isn't it?" she whispered.

"Yes," he whispered back, thinking they could be speaking of more than one thing.

"Why does it seem so special? Watching her sleep?"

"I don't know actually."

But it did. It seemed incredibly pure, the sight of it causing a catch in his heart. Yet the feeling? There was no explaining it.

Closing the bedroom door partway, they sauntered back into the family room, hand in hand. Candles still shimmered on the coffee table, casting a capricious, mystical glow about the room.

"I hope she's not fussy tomorrow when we take her for her picture with Santa."

"She'll be fine, I'm sure." He paused thoughtfully. "Though I'd pack the Tylenol for good measure."

Then as thoughts of baby matters retreated momentarily from the forefront of their minds, he settled into the overstuffed chair, pulling her along with him. She spilled into his lap, squealing at the impromptu gesture.

"And what about you, miss? What would you like from dear old Santa?"

"Me?" She grinned delightedly into his eyes. "I can't think of a thing."

"Really now? How is that?"

"I already have everything."

"You do?"

She put her arms around his neck. "I think I do," she said breathlessly, questioning him with her eyes.

He wanted to reassure her, answer her with a kiss. But the closeness of her snuggled against him became far too intoxicating. The scent of her something he wanted to revel in. If he kissed her now, he feared he'd never be able to stop.

"Do you have a Chia pet?" he asked inanely, going from the sublime to the ridiculous. Anything to cool his tempted senses.

She giggled. "A what?"

"A Chia pet."

"Not the last time I looked."

"Then I suppose you don't have everything, do you?"

"Hmm," she smiled, "and here I thought I was all set, my fortune complete."

"Ah, that's it. Perhaps we should consult the wisdom of the fortune cookies."

"Um, I already did," she confessed.

"Both of them?"

She nodded.

He straightened, peering down his nose at her. "Do we know each other well enough for that? Two kisses within the last thirty days and you're already reading my fortune cookies?" he teased. "You bold American girl, you."

"What ever are you going to do with me?"

He rolled his eyes toward the ceiling. "I suppose I'll just suffer through," he said, making her laugh. "So tell me. What did your fortune say?"

"Mine?"

He nodded. "Yours," he uttered, trying to tear his eyes from her lips as she spoke.

"Uh . . . mine said, 'Beware of strangers with foreign accents.' "

"Slightly paranoid, don't you think? Besides, it didn't say dashing, romantically-inclined strangers with foreign accents, did it?"

She chuckled and shook her head. "No, just strangers."

"See there, then it can't possibly be talking about me, can it?" He gave her a cocky, facetious grin. "And what, Nosy, did my fortune say?"

Shrugging, she told him matter-of-factly, "Something silly about finding romance in your furnace."

"My furnace?" he shrieked.

"That's what it said." She giggled. "But I think it was a typo."

"What do you think it was supposed to say?"

"Future. 'Look to find romance in your future.' "

"Marvelously clever, the Chinese." He smiled. "Excellent fortunetellers, don't you think? Actually," he suddenly found himself staring at her intently without really meaning to, "what *do* you think?"

He thought he knew what she was feeling in her heart. Hadn't she said as much today on the snowy golf course? He conjured up the scene once more, replaying her words in his mind. Could he have misconstrued her words, put too much weight on their kiss?

He didn't think so, but he'd hate to press himself on her if their feelings weren't totally mutual. And if she needed more time, that was fine, too. Patience was a virtue he'd learned well since moving to Somersby and meeting the incomparable Samantha Stevenson.

"I think . . ." she hesitated. "Could you give me five minutes? I'd like to change my sweater. All day out in the cold, you know. And then Emma splashed some of her cereal on me earlier. And a complete dropper full of Tylenol dripped on me, too. And, well, I'd just feel better if I—"

"Say no more." Placing his hands around her waist, he helped to hoist her up from his lap and the chair.

She disappeared into the bathroom, and soon after he heard the sink water running.

Could be more than five minutes . . .

Too anxious for her return to sit still, he packed up the leftover food and deposited it into the refrigerator. Then he carried their dishes out to the kitchen. Broken pieces of fortune cookies lay on Sam's plate. Picking up the white slips of paper splashed with red ink, he read them both.

"High fences make good neighbors," he murmured to himself. "Hills are steeper when standing at the bottom."

No mention of romance on either of them. The thought made him smile.

Ah, love is grand, isn't it?

He sat down once again, on the couch this time, his hands behind his head. Listening to her movements in her bedroom, he relished the moment she'd return to him. Closing his eyes, he imagined her next to him, reliving the kiss they'd shared that afternoon, thinking of all the ways he'd to try make her his tonight.

Chapter Twelve

Sam knew she was somewhat overdressed for a trip to the mall to see Santa, but it seemed like such a momentous occasion. And, admittedly, she wanted to look nice for Blake too. That's why she'd chosen her long black skirt and boots, topped with a Christmas-red shell and black hooded sweater trimmed with faux ebony fur.

But nothing could compare to the natural beauty of the baby girl she'd just dressed, and she couldn't help but gaze upon her with astonished adoration.

"You are the most beautiful creature of all," she sighed at Emma, holding the baby's waving fists in her own.

Aunt Maria had bought Emma a precious outfit for the special occasion—a white knit double-breasted sweater with hood, trimmed in pink with pastel songbirds embroidered on either side at the bottom. It came with white knit, footed pants trimmed in pink, too, and a tiny pink velcro bow for Emma's wisps of blonde hair.

Emma's sky blue eyes sparkled at the soft-spoken

compliment, and for a moment, Sam could have sworn she glimpsed a bit of heaven in them. She wondered at the day that Emma could speak back to her, imagined the talks they'd share, the laughter they'd enjoy together.

Overwhelmed by her feelings, she sighed once again. "I love you so much, little girl," she said, picking up the child and hugging her close to her heart.

The doorbell rang just then, and Sam knew it had to be Blake. It was slightly earlier than they had agreed on, but then maybe he was anxious. Last evening hadn't exactly gone as planned after all. By the time she'd gotten cleaned up and changed, Blake had fallen asleep on her family room couch!

It seemed pointless to wake him. Especially since, somehow in her mind, it seemed they'd have many future evenings to share together. Instead, she had snuggled up against him and dozed peacefully herself, satiated with all the love and happiness her heart could hold. An hour or so later, they roused, made plans for the morning, and kissed goodnight.

"Coming!" she called out, eagerly making her way to the front door. *Does this mean he's as anxious to see me as I am to see him?*

In her typical manner of greeting, she opened the door holding Emma in her arms, a spontaneous smile bursting across her face. "A little early, aren't you?"

A snowy-white world glistening under bright December sunlight, greeted her back, nearly blinding her. She blinked several times, trying to focus. There appeared to be two forms standing on her snow-laden doorstep.

Squinting into the brightness she ventured, "Brittany?"

She couldn't believe her former intern was standing there.

"Brittany and—" She glanced at the other shadowy shape. "Justin?"

A glittery ring on Brittany's left hand sparkled at the corner of Sam's vision. Sam blinked again. Tried to keep her voice steady.

"Come in, you two."

Like a whip of winter air, Blake blustered into the family room where Sam stood holding Emma, his cheeks crimson from the cold.

"Sorry to burst in unannounced, but I was knocking and—" He paused, his eyes seeming to light up with awe and pride at the sight of them. "My!" he exclaimed. "How stunning my two girls look!"

Then, apparently sensing the quiet presence of the college-aged couple seated on the couch, he turned to them and apologized.

"Please forgive me." He extended his hand toward the young man. "I'm Blake. Blake Dawson."

"Justin." The sandy-haired young man reached out to grasp his hand. "Talbot," he added as Blake turned to the young woman.

"Brittany." She nodded politely.

"Brittany?" A note of recognition crept into Blake's voice. "Sam's intern from years past? The one whom she still speaks so fondly of?"

"I guess so," the girl said quietly.

"Wonderful!" He clapped his hands. "Wonderful meeting both of you, and please forgive me for being rude. I didn't mean to break in on your visit, but I get a bit over zealous at times, especially on days such as this." He turned his attention to Emma, who sat smiling in Sam's arms, apparently tickled by all the commotion going on around her.

"This is a big day for us, isn't it, darling?" He tickled the baby girl under her chin.

"We're going to visit Santa Claus," he explained jovially to the two college students. "Obviously not to ask for any presents. She doesn't need a bicycle or a make-up kit yet." He laughed. "No, we're just going to get a photo with Santa, aren't we, love? And maybe a glossy with an elf, too?" he cooed to the baby.

She waved her fists at him, and he smiled as one of her hands found his finger and encircled it. "Emma's first visit to Santa. A very big day to be sure. Perhaps we'll even have several copies of the photo made to give to our parents. Sounds like a plan, I think."

Glancing up, he seemed to suddenly realize no one was joining in on his prattle. Instead, Sam and the young couple were all staring at him solemnly.

"Something's wrong." His voice held the slightest hint of a question.

He stood still, studying the three adults around him.

"Something's very wrong . . ." he said more assuredly this time.

"Blake—" Sam's voice cracked, just as she knew it would if she tried to speak. Tears began to flow onto her cheeks—but words were too challenging, wouldn't come.

"Sam, love, what is it? Did you have a rough night?"

Tightening her hold on the baby, she shook her head vehemently.

Obviously puzzled, Blake glanced at the couple for an explanation. But they sat closely together, united and silent.

Sam watched through tear-blurred eyes as his gaze swept over the couple, assessing the situation as quickly as he gleaned a legal document.

The signs were all there. A shiny new ring. The somber aura that hovered around them. The anxious look on their faces. Jason's head of light hair. Brittany's bright blue eyes—the same shade as Emma's.

"Oh, my God." His shoulders crumpled. "Oh my God, no." He shook his head in denial. "Not now—not ever." His eyes pleading, he looked to Justin first. "Are you sure?"

The younger man stared at him wordlessly, a youthful apprehension, a tinge of defiance marking his expression. But Brittany couldn't look him in the eyes, her glance downcast, turned away.

Blake turned to Sam. "Sam?"

Through her own tears, she saw the moisture forming in his eyes. Eyes that were usually so playful, mischievous, full of life. Now so forlorn, it broke her heart all over again.

Is this what knowing me has done to him?

"Oh, Blake!" she cried out.

He went to her, wrapping his arms around her and the precious Emma. She fell into the comfort of his arms, leaning her head on his shoulder. "I hoped and I prayed . . ." he said, weeping along with her. "It just . . . wasn't enough. Only a little more time, a little more time and perhaps . . ."

She already knew the words he left unspoken. It was the same wish she'd carried in her heart every moment of every day, for every month Emma had been a part of her life. Had become her life.

Crushed together by their sorrow and love, they held

onto each other tightly, wrapped in a hug that had to last a lifetime. As always, Emma was at the center of their love. This time, she cried out so as not to be smothered by it.

Blake took a step back, but just a step. Just enough to give Emma room to breathe. But he kept his eyes on the baby girl, and one arm around Sam as if he could shield her from any more pain.

"We didn't mean to cause all of this, you know." The baby's whimpering seemed to give Justin courage enough to speak up. "But we've missed Corinne . . ."

"Corinne?" Blake turned to face him, his lawyer's voice somewhat challenging.

Justin's mouth twitched. "Our baby."

Blake nodded feebly. "Yes . . . of course . . . ," he whispered.

But he wasn't looking at Justin now; he was staring into Sam's eyes—questioning her, searching her curiously for their next move. But she didn't have any answers. All she knew was that she couldn't do it. She couldn't be the one to hand the baby girl over to her father. Or even to the baby's mother, though Brittany was a person she cared for deeply.

Instead, though she knew it wasn't right to put the final burden on Blake, she handed Emma to him.

As always, he seemed more than happy to take the darling infant into his strong, capable hands. And for a moment—a tenuous fantasy of a moment—Sam imagined that he might take the baby they loved and shared, and run to the ends of the earth with her.

Blake Dawson always saves the day, doesn't he?

Maybe he could run fast, run hard. So far away . . . to some hidden place where Sam could meet them both . . .

and the three of them would live as a family . . . happily ever after.

But instead, he seemed paralyzed. Transfixed, standing there gazing down at the baby in his arms while Sam slumped helplessly into the closest chair, watching them through the rivulets of tears that wouldn't stop.

"My princess . . ." he whispered hoarsely. "My darling princess . . ."

His voice was the only thing to be heard in the quiet of the room. Without looking at the young couple, he spoke to them.

"Funny story . . ." He sniffled, the slightest fragment of a poignant smile touching his lips. "That first day . . . we didn't know the baby's name . . . didn't know your name, did we, bugaboo?"

As always, Emma responded to his term of endearment with a delighted gurgle. At the sound, a sob escaped him, and he paused momentarily, attempting to gather his composure once more.

"We went to a diner . . . and the waitress asked her name . . . because, you know . . . she's so beautiful . . ." His shoulders began to shake, and his head hung down over his broken heart. "So beautiful . . ."

And then, just like Sam, the tears he wept seemed to rob him of his capacity to speak. Without another word, he handed the baby girl over to her father.

Chapter Thirteen

"**I** think there's been a misunderstanding."

Even weeks later, sitting at her desk at the agency, Sam could still hear the words Justin had spoken just moments after Blake settled Emma into the young father's arms. She could still feel how her heart had sunk to the depths of hell . . . and then caught in her chest at the sound of his words. Lodging there, afraid to soar with hope—but longing to do so.

In fact, even now she could picture the college boy seated on her couch holding Emma a bit stiffly. He had hardly looked old enough to be married, let alone be comfortable with the responsibility of caring for an infant. A look of consternation had etched his soft, barely whiskered face while his fiancée, on the other hand, brightened as she focused on the baby.

Taking the baby from Justin's awkward embrace, Brittany had seemed uninterested in the tense dynamics going on around her. Instead, she rocked Emma, whispering to her sweetly, looking natural—though still far too young—in the maternal role.

In retrospect, Sam figured she must have looked just as confused as Justin did. She had glanced at Blake trying to gauge his take on the situation, but he only blinked at her with perplexed, shadowed eyes. Like her, he seemed bewildered, not sure what to think of Justin's statement. Like her, he appeared to hold his breath while Justin recounted the turmoil he and his bride-to-be had been through the past year.

Apparently, the young couple had almost split up when they'd learned of the pregnancy. At least Brittany had thought they should part. Justin was heartbroken, and it took a while before he realized Brittany was only trying to be brave for his benefit, trying to take on the unexpected burden herself so he could keep his mind on college.

"But I couldn't forget about her—the baby, I mean," Justin confessed to Sam and Blake. "I'd loved Brittany since we were in high school. I've always known she was the one. No one else makes me laugh like she does, and well—I couldn't stick her with a problem we both created, you know?"

Ultimately, they set up prenatal appointments with an obstetrician close to campus, and Justin made sure he accompanied Brittany to every one of them. But there was also the issue of additional money, they realized. Brittany sold some of her jewelry and Justin worked extra shifts at Taco Casa so they could afford to buy the things they knew they'd need once the baby arrived: an infant carrier, blankets, diapers and so on. Neither Brittany nor Justin wanted to ask their parents for extra help or cash since their families were already financing their college.

"Pretty much we'd gotten ourselves into this, and we thought we should get ourselves out," he explained.

They figured they only had to keep it together for the nine months of the pregnancy, and then . . . well, then after a while they could drop off the baby to someone who would take care of him or her, someone nurturing and loving.

"Naturally, Brittany thought of you," Justin told Sam, making her spirits lift again. "And then when we heard you were engaged to a millionaire," he half-smiled, "well, we felt like we'd hit the jackpot where the baby was concerned."

"And when you heard I was no longer engaged?" Sam couldn't help from asking.

At the question, Brittany had spoken up. "A friend of mind from home sent me newspaper articles. You and the baby seemed to be in the Somersby Chronicles quite a lot for a while there. You looked so happy. I knew, married or single, you'd love our baby no matter what."

"So the bottom line is . . ." Blake urged the couple to get to the point. Though atypical for him, Sam could sense his frustration, his growing impatience.

"Bottom line is, uh—" Justin paused, sat up straighter, then bent forward, his elbows on his knees. Wringing his hands together till it seemed they'd fall off, he cleared his throat before answering. "Well, we plan on getting married two years from now. But honestly, we know we're too young to have a child. We have too much school in front of us. Too much growing up to do. We'd, uh, like it a lot—appreciate it," he turned to Sam, his hands finally still, "if you could adopt our baby girl. I mean, we'd still like to visit her from time to time. We want her to know—" he hesitated, his face reddening, his voice faltering.

Brittany pulled the baby closer to her, interjecting in a soft voice, "We want her to know she had parents who loved her enough to give her up."

Blake glanced at Sam then, and with the unspoken communication they shared, she read the overwhelming relief in his eyes. She also knew, as he seemed to realize, that this was a painfully difficult time for the young couple. Being the elders in the situation, they needed to be respectful of that fact, even if their first inclination was to whoop with joy. Pure joy!

Even now, Sam's eyes welled up a bit thinking of how she felt at that precise moment. Her resurgence of happy tears transformed April into a slightly blurry image as she entered Sam's office.

"Special delivery," her assistant said perkily, handing Sam an open express mail package. "It's the Korneffel adoption papers you've been waiting for." She straightened the fuzzy red-and-white Santa Claus hat angled on her head before continuing. "I'll tell you what," she put her hands on her slim hips, hitching her fingers onto the belt loops of her red and gold paisley pants, "I can't wait till one of those arrives with your name on it. I don't mean to sound nosy, but when is Julia Theodore going to have your adoption papers ready?"

Sam smiled. April really never did mean to be nosy or impertinent. She was just so full of curiosity, so anxious to know the outcomes of things that she couldn't help herself. That's why she always read the last page of her paperback novels first.

"Julia promised to turn it around as quickly as she

could. I'm expecting us to see it after the holidays." Sam included April in the upcoming occasion. "Speaking of holidays, weren't you supposed to be off today?"

"I was, but since you came in . . ." April shrugged her narrow shoulders.

"You didn't have to come in because of me, April. I'm sure you have a zillion last minute things to do."

"Someone has to push you out the door."

Sam lifted the chunk of a document April had just delivered to her. "I promised I'd expedite this, make sure it's ready before the first of the year."

"Well, there's still the week after Christmas for that. Besides, don't you have a date with that charming Englishman of yours tomorrow night?"

"Tomorrow night, yes." Sam nodded with a grin, amused by April's concern. "But that's more than twenty-four hours from now."

"So? You should get out of here anyway. Go have your nails done or something while Emma is at your aunt's."

Sam squinted at April quizzically. Earthy April rarely spent time in salons of any sort. "I've never had my nails done."

"It'll be a Christmas present to yourself then," April urged. "Don't you want your hands to look nice for the holidays?"

"I'd never really thought about it."

"Well, maybe you should."

With that, April picked up the framed picture of Emma with Santa from the growing collection of baby photos adorning Sam's desk.

"She is so adorable," her assistant sighed dreamily. "Emma Corinne. I love that name."

One at a time, April plucked several more photos from Sam's desk, studying them with admiration. Some were solely of Emma, a couple others featured Emma with Sam, and a few captured Blake and Emma. None depicted Sam and Blake together.

"Have the two of you—you and Mr. Dawson—ever been alone?" April asked.

"Without Em in the next room?"

April nodded.

"Uh, no," Sam answered her.

"Well, Merry Christmas and Happy New Year then!" April shouted jubilantly. "Tomorrow night will be your first time?" Her assistant's eyes lit up. "Christmas Eve! How romantic!"

I had hoped, Sam sighed. She'd been looking forward to their date for weeks, but the closer it got, the more stressed she felt. And not because she was anxious about leaving Emma. No. More like because she hadn't talked to Blake for days. He used to call every morning, or drop in to spend the evening with her and Emma, but suddenly he'd been missing in action. She'd tried to call him, but hadn't gotten an answer. She'd left messages, but he hadn't returned her calls. Her stomach fluttered nervously at the thought.

April interrupted her worries. "What are you planning to do?"

"Excuse me?"

"Your date—what are you planning to do?"

"Well, we're supposed to have dinner and then go to midnight service at that historic church in Mt. Adams, at the top of the hill."

But they'd made those plans over a week ago. Maybe he had changed his mind. Maybe he just wasn't interested in her anymore. Maybe he never really had been. Maybe she'd imagined it all. Or maybe he was just busy from the holidays? Could that be it? Maybe?

"Maybe you'll be doing this regularly from now on," April chirped up.

Or maybe not. Sam sighed again.

"Ryan and I can watch Emma Corinne," April stressed the name, "anytime you want. Are Maria and Dom already on for tomorrow night?"

Sam nodded. "I'll be off all day so they'll only have her for an evening shift. Uncle Dom is so excited. He plans on reading *The Night Before Christmas* to her—though she won't understand a word."

"Meanwhile," April looked wistful, "you'll be having dinner for two followed by a candlelight service. It sounds perfect!" She put her stamp of approval on the plans before turning and heading back to her desk.

Probably back to her *True Romance* or her horoscope, Sam surmised.

If only my life was that simple!

She had thought once the fear of losing Emma vanished that everything in her life would be perfect. But now . . . well, now she was afraid she was losing Blake. He'd sure been acting strange this week. Not as attentive as usual. She'd only seen him for a couple of hours at the very beginning of the week. And even then he seemed unusually secretive. Whenever his cell phone rang, he'd glance at the number then stick it back in his pocket hurriedly with no explanation.

Maybe he'd met someone else. Someone he wanted to get to know better? After all, just because you walk into a guy's office one morning carrying an abandoned baby doesn't mean he has to fall in love with you. And even if he does become enamored by the situation, it doesn't mean his feelings have to stay that way. They'd only shared a couple of kisses here and there. It wasn't like promises of true love or anything.

And really, if she were totally honest, his reaction that day with Justin and Brittany *had* always nagged at her. True, she and Blake had both behaved irrationally, jumping to conclusions the way that they had, their emotions out of control. But still, she couldn't help but wonder . . . would he have acted that distraught if *she* were missing from his life?

Sam removed the adoption packet from the legal-sized envelope, wanting nothing more than to bury herself in her work for a few more hours. But instead, the legal document only reminded her of more loose ends, more questions.

No doubt she really couldn't wait until Emma became legally hers. But, somehow she kept thinking Blake would say something, anything, about wanting to be a part of it too.

Okay, apparently from the way he'd been acting lately it was doubtful he wanted to share a parenting role with her. But wouldn't he want to be some sort of guardian backup? At the very least, a godfather?

It would seem odd not to have the Englishman be a part of Emma's life. He'd been there from the start— from within the first hour Sam laid eyes on the baby and had taken her to Blake's office. She and Blake had named the infant, taken her to her first doctor's appointment, rejoiced in her first smiles, coddled her through teething pains, paced the floor with her during tummy aches.

Blake had taken Emma home with him some nights,

his shoulder weighted down with an overloaded diaper bag, so Sam could have an evening off and get a good night's rest. In return, Sam would sometimes run to his place early in the morning to make breakfast for the two of them. All in all, they'd held the baby girl close to their hearts, gladly revolved their lives around her, and loved her like their own.

But that doesn't mean he has to be in love with me, she reminded herself painfully. *And he doesn't have to be in love with me . . . just because I'm in love with him.*

She knew for a fact that quite often, in intense or passionate situations, couples who were thrown together didn't always stay together. Many times they drifted apart once the problem or issue got resolved, no melodrama left to bind them.

An upsetting thought to be sure. Hopefully, that wouldn't happen to her and Blake.

Or had it already?

Suddenly the task of looking over the adoption papers seemed overwhelming, daunting. Perhaps April was right. It was time to call it quits, go pick up Emma from Aunt Maria's, and start thinking Christmas. She had all next week to work on the document. No matter what, she'd have it ready on time as promised.

Opening her desk drawer, she dug through the mess in search of an oversized rubber band to hold the packet together. Papers spilled out of the desk, and she leaned over her chair to pick them up.

Prescott Sterling.

The name jumped up from one of the papers, her old pros and cons list, startling her like a prowler sneaking up from behind.

Wow. It was hard to believe there had actually been

a time in her life that a relationship like the one she and Prescott shared could've possibly seemed like enough for her. It seemed like another lifetime ago that he'd even been a consideration—and at least that long since lists and words on paper dictated the course of her life.

Now her mind, led by her heart, ruled her decisions. And she hoped as Uncle Dom had said, they would see her through—because right now, this minute, her heart was aching to hear Blake's voice.

With Prescott she'd written bland, contained words to express her feelings for him, all so superficial. How she realized now that they lacked any true emotion.

PROS
Decent looking, good height
Kind and diplomatic—esp.
with his widowed mother
Nice smile, good orthodontia work
Financially sound
Wants to wait to be intimate till
wedding night

But with Blake, she could barely think of words that adequately described her feelings for him. It didn't even matter that he was the most incredible looking man she'd ever laid eyes on. It was everything about him that she loved so much. The way that dark lock of hair sometimes fell on his forehead. How his eyes gleamed mischievously, deliciously, as if he were in on all of life's little secrets. It was his hands that could calm with a touch. His lips, exciting and delighting beyond belief with even the most tender kiss.

His laughter made her smile even when she didn't

think anything was funny. His arms were the one place in the world where she had felt most at home. Yet—why was she torturing herself this way? It certainly didn't help. Didn't make her feel any better. It only made her realize how much she truly loved the Englishman.

Chapter Fourteen

Sam followed the scent of baking cookies into the haven of her aunt's kitchen. A hint of cinnamon hung in the air, mixing with the aromatic pine from wreaths and garlands strung all through the house. For a moment, she basked in the familiar comfort of holiday coziness that enveloped her.

"How are you two ladies?"

She smiled at her aunt who sat in a padded cherry wood chair feeding Emma a bottle. Little Em's eyes were wide open, her arms moving excitedly as she sucked. Sam leaned over, brushing the baby's soft forehead with a light kiss, a feeling of gratitude causing her heart to swell. No matter what else, she was so lucky to have this precious angel in her life.

"We've had a great day, haven't we, princess?" Her aunt smiled at the baby and then at Sam.

"That's always good to hear." Sam paused, sniffing the air around her. "Snickerdoodles, right?"

Aunt Maria nodded. "Your Christmas favorite."

158

Sam plucked a chocolate sandwich cookie with a red icing middle from a snowman dish on the kitchen's island then took a seat across from Emma and her aunt. "You did a great job on these too," she said, testing her aunt's batch from the previous day.

Aunt Maria glowed from the compliment. Though actually, Sam considered, her aunt seemed to glow all the time now. While Maria's offer to take care of Emma had been a godsend for Sam, it seemed to suit the older woman quite well, too. Maria took delight in everything Emma did, always full of smiles at day's end. After all her aunt and uncle had done for her, Sam felt pleased she could provide this bit of unexpected happiness in their lives.

"Miss Emma tried a few bites of carrots today," her aunt informed her.

Sam wrinkled her nose. "Did she like it?"

"Not as well as the sweet potatoes yesterday. But overall, I'd say she's enjoying her new food ventures. Would you like to finish feeding her, honey?" she deferred to Sam. "The cookies are about to come out."

"That's okay. You two look perfectly content. I'll tend to the cookies." She glanced at the timer on the stove, which had only seconds to go.

"You'll never guess what else your little one did today." Her aunt beamed with a proud, smug smile, making Sam chuckle.

"Something incredible I'm sure, since she *is* the most incredible baby in the whole wide world."

Her aunt nodded agreeably. "She sat up. All by herself."

"Em! You sat up!" Sam clapped her hands together. No wonder her aunt was glowing.

"Not for long, of course," Maria assured her. "She toppled over after a few seconds. But, I couldn't believe it. Already she's trying to sit up."

The timer buzzed and Sam sprung up from the chair, grabbing an oven mitt. Her spirits felt far lighter than they had when she first walked in the door.

"Blake called moments after it happened," her aunt talked on. "I hope you don't mind, but I was so excited I blabbed all about it."

The blast of hot oven air hit her face at the same time his name reached her ears. Both jarred her, the cookie sheet faltering in her hands. Snickerdoodles went sliding, almost spilling onto the floor. She salvaged the tray of cookies only by chance.

"Blake called?" Shocked, she stood holding the oven-hot cookie sheet in her hand. "He called here?"

"He calls every day. Well, almost every day. Just to check in on Em and me."

"Oh." Her mouth gaped. "I mean, I knew he called once in a while. But this week? He's been calling all this week?"

Maria nodded. "He's such an adorable man, isn't he?" Her aunt's voice took on that pleasurable trill common to all women who came in contact with him.

Sam placed the cookie sheet on top of the stove, then bent down to close the oven door, a sick feeling flowing from her stomach into the back of her throat.

Just because I'm in love with him . . . doesn't mean he has to be in love with me. The saddening mantra resounded in her mind.

"So you two are still planning on going out tomorrow night?"

"He said that?" Sam grasped for any shred of information. No way she wanted to share her doubts with Aunt Maria. No way she wanted her aunt to be disappointed or worried.

"Actually he asked if your uncle and I were still planning on watching Em."

Was he trying to get out of it? Hoping they would be suddenly unavailable?

"And you said . . ."

"Yes, of course."

"And he said . . ."

Her aunt seemed to hesitate, to flush. "Oh, I can't remember exactly. Something charming, I'm sure."

"I'm sure."

Sam removed the oven mitt, and took a spatula from a nearby kitchen drawer. The cookies had cooled long enough to be moved from the cookie sheet.

On the counter, next to the oven, there was a sparkling glass platter etched with the form of a sister and brother in their winter nightclothes, holding hands, staring out a frosty window at Santa and his reindeer flying through the night sky.

How she'd hoped of having a little brother or sister for Emma to grow up with . . .

"You want the cookies on this platter, right?"

Her aunt nodded as she propped Emma over her shoulder to burp her. "Thank you, honey." She patted Emma's back. "Do you know what you're wearing tomorrow evening? Something festive?"

"I hadn't thought much about it," Sam fibbed, as she slid the cookies onto the dish.

In reality, she'd been through everything in her closet and out shopping on her lunch hour several times trying to find the perfect outfit—something special for what she had thought would be a special occasion.

Finally, she'd decided on something burgundy, thinking it looked good with her hair. The lightweight burgundy sweater had a flattering scooped neck, trimmed in a sheer burgundy lace around the neckline and three-quarter length sleeves. The matching, slim-fitting velvet skirt had a simple, but eye-catching floral design done with silver thread and clusters of onyx beads. It was an elegant outfit, but perhaps she'd take it all back to the store and save the money.

"Going to have your nails done?"

Spatula in hand, Sam turned to give her aunt a puzzled look. "My nails? Why does everyone seem to have a sudden interest in my nails?"

"Oh, well," her aunt stammered, apparently flustered. "It's nothing. Nothing, dear. Just a question. Thought you might want to make your nails look nice, that's all. You have such pretty hands," she added lamely.

That wasn't quite true. Her hands were dry. Her nails were chipped. But at this point, no word from Blake, did it really matter? Who cared?

She grabbed a Snickerdoodle from the platter. Maybe she'd eat the entire plateful. Gain five extra pounds. *Maybe that will make me feel better.*

"Samantha, honey," Maria interrupted her private pity party. "Could you please take Emma for a moment? Mother Nature is calling."

Laying the cookie down on the counter, Sam stretched out her arms. "Come here, little girl." Taking the baby from her aunt, she snuggled Emma against her. "I've missed you," she told Em as Maria retreated from the kitchen.

As always, one look at Emma's shining, wide eyes and sweet face and all her concerns seemed to magically subside for the moment. The weight of the world lifted while the weight of Emma, her precious bundle, felt soothing and wonderfully right in her arms.

"Have you seen all the pretty Christmas things?" she whispered to the infant, carrying her into the family room.

A blue-gold fire crackled in the fireplace, adding an extra shimmer to the already sparkling holiday decorations placed all throughout the space. Wreathed candles and glass containers with glittery ornaments graced tabletops. Baskets set on the floor brimmed with stuffed Santas and snowmen. Sprays of evergreen, tied with ribbons and pinecones, decked the walls.

"Oh, look at that." Sam pointed to the top of the fresh Douglas fir tree filling the corner of the room. "That's an angel. Kind of like you. Only you don't have wings."

Emma seemed to coo at the remark, so Sam prattled on, "Aunt Maria told me her mother gave her that angel many, many years ago. Maybe I'll give you a Christmas angel someday. Would you like that?"

The strings of Christmas tree lights were turned on, and Aunt Maria had Christmas music playing so softly in the background Sam hadn't even heard it at first. The lyrics of the carols . . . the enchanting delights of the season all seemed to hold more meaning than ever with Emma cradled against her.

"And did you see this?" Her eyes gazed over the ornaments on the tree until she found the pale pink bulb with a miniature manger scene painted on it. "Know what it says?" She glanced at Emma. " 'Baby's First Christmas.' Baby, meaning you. Your Aunt Maria and

Uncle Dom bought that for you because they're so glad you're here. Isn't that sweet?"

Emma let out a giggly gurgle, her hands reaching out to touch the fragile keepsake.

"And what else does Aunt Maria have for us to look at?"

Sam turned to the fireplace where garlands of long-needle pine dressed up the mantel and flowed down each side, the finishing touch of a red velvety bow placed at each corner. A golden Christmas star glowed from the center of the display, flanked by an assortment of framed family photos.

Sam felt the warmth of the fire on her legs as she leaned in to get a closer look at all the smiling faces there.

"There's Aunt Maria when she was a little girl," she said, pointing to an antique oval frame. "And this is a picture of your Grandma and Grandpa Stevenson with Aunt Maria and Uncle Dom," she nodded to a photo of the foursome. "That's when they were all much younger."

"Oh, and—" she chuckled out loud, picking up a silver-plated frame. "Here's a picture of me in high school. What was I thinking with that hair style?" She rolled her eyes at Emma before setting the photo back down in its spot.

Shifting her feet, she moved over to get a better look at the last photo sitting on the shelf. "Oh my gosh, Em, this is you. You. And me. And . . ." Her voice softened, "Blake."

She'd forgotten that Uncle Dom had his camera out on Thanksgiving, taking pictures of all the family members gathered together. She'd never seen the photo before. As far as Sam knew, it was the only existing picture of the three of them together.

A rush of memories assaulted her as she stood staring at it. And a gush of feelings too. Everything had been so perfect that day.

Well, that wasn't totally true.

I wasn't sure how long you'd be with me, Sam hugged the baby to her chest. *And I wanted to keep you so much.*

But now that that fear had been put to rest, it seemed easy to recall all the wonderful things that had taken place that afternoon. Seeing her parents together, in the same room, both enjoying Emma so much. Getting to meet members of Blake's family. Observing the happiness that danced in her aunt and uncle's eyes that day. And then Blake . . .

Did I imagine it? She stared harder at the photo, trying to find an answer there.

He had seemed so interested. Even talking futuristically, she recalled, teasing about their baking contest the next year . . . smiling about making her mom a lifelong fan.

Oh, I sound like a silly schoolgirl!

Those weren't exactly promises of happily ever after, by any means. Especially not from someone like Blake who was eager to please, anxious to set everyone's world right. She'd known he was a charmer since the moment they'd first met. No doubt he was just being his undeniably engaging self.

And, anyway, the reason he *seemed* interested was totally clear. He was—in Emma anyway. That was evident, documented in Kodak color in fact, right before her eyes. The way he held Emma on his lap possessively, his arms protective, his smile so proud and unrestrained.

Any stranger would be able to see how much he loved that little girl, how happy he was to hold her close to him, be a part of her life.

A part of Emma's life . . .

Sam glanced at the infant, and an overwhelming feeling of love burned in her chest.

Emma deserved that, didn't she? She deserved to have a man as wonderful as Blake in her life. Someone who cared about her as much as he did. A person who had been there from the very start. Every little girl needed that, needed all the love, encouragement and adoration she could get from as many people as she could. And this little girl, given the circumstances, even more so.

So it's up to me to be a big girl, Sam sighed.

As perfect as the photo of the three of them looked, as much as she wanted that to be the way they walked through life, as much as she loved him . . .

If it turned out that Blake just wanted to be friends, well, then . . .

It will be okay . . .

Though her heart wrenched in reluctance, it would be okay. It would have to be okay . . . for Emma's sake.

"For you, I can handle it," she whispered to the baby girl.

I'll put on my new outfit. She vowed silently. *I'll be gracious and attentive to him.*

"I promise," she murmured.

Kissing Emma's forehead, the baby girl seemed to smile up at her as if pleased with her decision. As always, the look melted Sam's heart. "Okay, okay, you win," Sam conceded. "I'll even do my nails."

Chapter Fifteen

$\mathbf{S}$am stopped in the middle of folding Emma's onesie t-shirts piled on top of the clothes dryer, straining to hear over the sloshing washing machine.

"Em. Listen!"

Startled, Emma looked up. Her favorite toy, a stuffed wiggle worm, stopped in mid-wave in her hand.

"It's Blake," Sam exclaimed, dropping the tee instantly.

It had to be him. It didn't sound like Uncle Dom. And what other man would be leaving a message on her phone machine?

Picking up Emma's infant carrier, she hustled them both down the hall to the phone in the kitchen.

She pushed the stop button on the message machine, and answered the phone, hoping she merely sounded out of breath. No way she'd ever want him to know how truly anxious she felt.

"Hello?"

Her heart was racing, not knowing what to expect

from him. Would he still want to go out tonight? Did he still want to be part of their lives? At least Emma's?

"Hey. I didn't think you were home. Did I catch you at a bad time?"

Did I catch you at a bad time?

Her mind worked double-time, playing back the words, hearing the voice all over again. Then . . .

. . . all hope flowed out of her. Her heart stopped racing. Instead it just plain sank. The voice definitely didn't belong to Blake.

"I think you have the wrong number," she told the caller.

"Isn't this Samantha Stevenson?" the man asked.

"Yes. But I'm not sure who you are," she admitted, though the more the man spoke, the more familiar the voice seemed.

"You probably didn't hear the first part of my message. It's Tom."

"Tom?" She glanced at Emma and shrugged her shoulders.

"Chief McKnight."

"Oh." Her stomach tightened as she set Emma's carrier on the kitchen table. Instantly her legs felt wobbly, and she sank down into one of the oak chairs. "Is—is something wrong?"

Her eyes swept over Emma who was still playing with her toy, oblivious to Sam's concern. He couldn't possibly be calling about Emma, could he? Had Brittany and Justin somehow changed their minds? Or had something happened to her aunt . . . her uncle . . . Blake?

"That's usually the reaction I get from everyone." His chuckle was a deep baritone. "But, no, nothing's wrong," he told her, then paused giving her ample time to heave a sigh of relief. "And actually that's kind of why I'm calling."

"Oh?" she responded again.

"I don't have many cases that end like yours, Miss Stevenson. I just wanted to congratulate you."

"Well, thanks," she replied, surprised.

"Yeah," he chuckled again, "you were bound and determined to keep that little girl, weren't you?"

His words brought a smile to her face, a smile that she directed at Emma, caressing the baby's cheek. "Yes, I'm really lucky it turned out this way."

"Sounds like she's lucky, too." There was a pause before he added contemplatively, "Yeah, a happy ending. Doesn't happen much in my line of work. Well . . . you all have a great holiday—make that a great New Year, you hear?"

"You, too, Chief McKnight," she replied automatically. But her mind was stuck on the words 'happy ending.' And her heart was wishing Blake were part of that happiness. "I'll bring Emma by sometime. You won't believe how much she's grown."

"That'd be great, Miss Stevenson. You all take good care now," he said, hanging up the phone before she could reply.

And before she could admit to herself that no matter how happy she was to have everything proceeding with Emma's adoption, Tom McKnight's voice was not the one she'd so hoped to hear.

Emma had fallen asleep in her car seat on the way home from running errands. Sam carried her into the house as quietly as she could, trying not to disturb the infant's afternoon slumber.

Making a path to the baby's room, she laid Em down amid the clusters of white lambs on the sky-blue flannel crib sheets. Untying Emma's knit hat, she lifted it off easily. Then ever so gently, tugged at the zipper on the baby's one-piece snowsuit, and worked to delicately remove that too.

Her hands were becoming more adept at dressing and undressing Em. But she never got used to some of the funny facial expressions Emma made especially when she interfered with any of Sleeping Beauty's trips to Dreamland. Clearly agitated, Emma would scrunch up her button nose and draw in her little bow of a mouth while keeping her eyes closed shut, tight as could be. She resembled a life-sized apple doll, and Sam had to work hard not to burst into giggles.

After covering Emma with a baby blanket, she headed back to the car, unloading the packages from the supermarket. Carrying them into the kitchen, she spotted the red blinking light on the message machine.

"I knew this would happen," she said out loud, depositing the packages onto the kitchen counter. She and Emma had only been gone an hour. But, of course, that's probably when Blake had called. She pushed the play button to see.

"Ah, so you two girls are out gallivanting, are you?"

She tried to put the groceries away while she nonchalantly listened to his message. Tried to keep her emotions in check as his voice, his presence, filled the room.

With robot-like motions, she put the milk in the refrigerator. "Actually I'm out, too."

Bread in the bread drawer. "Having a bit of a difficult time today, and I'm running behind."

Lettuce in the vegetable bin. "Would you mind meeting me at DeAngelo's tonight? I know it's not what we had planned . . ."

Baby food in the pantry. ". . . but I don't want us to be late for our reservations."

Dishwasher detergent under the sink. ". . . and I promise to explain later."

Eggs in the egg holder. "I've got to run. See you there."

Through it all, every word, she tried to pretend that he was just a friend she was meeting for dinner. Nothing more. But her heart couldn't be fooled. Neither could any other part of her body.

Hearing the Englishman again only made her long for him even more. Only made her want to reach out and touch the man behind that soothing, familiar voice. Only made her want to feel his touch again, too, his arms holding her close, his lips so soft on hers.

This isn't going to be easy. She rolled her eyes heavenward, seeking strength.

Hanging her coat over one of the kitchen chairs, she started to pull at the striped scarf around her neck. But instead she lifted the soft wool to her cheek, remembering the night Blake had given her the handmade gift . . . recalling how he'd wrapped it around her and pulled her close to him. So irresistibly close.

No, she'd leave the scarf on just for now. It made him seem nearby as she sat down with her new bottle of nail polish and began her preparations to meet her man friend for dinner, the man that she loved.

Chapter Sixteen

DeAngelo's was exquisite. Inside, hundreds of tiny white Christmas lights twinkled, all woven tastefully amid the Greek columns and ornamentation of the baroque décor. Outside the expansive windows, the view of the entire city was illuminated, too, glittering in excited anticipation of the holiday.

Off in the corner, the sweet pluckings of a violin and cello combined with a melodious piano and drifted through each nook of the restaurant, creating a tranquil, romantic ambience. As always, it was apparent the Englishman knew how to do things right.

"Would you like a glass of wine, Miss? Some coffee or tea while you're waiting?"

It was the second time the waiter had checked on Sam, doing his best to make her feel welcome, maybe even sensing her discomfort. Although she had dined alone many times at many restaurants over the years, tonight she did feel totally conspicuous. All dressed up in her new fancy outfit, sitting by herself at a table for two, at a four-star restaurant on Christmas Eve seemed awkward and humbling.

This time she took the waiter up on his offer.

"Hot tea would be wonderful, thank you," she replied gratefully, the mere thought warming her a bit. Her hands were, after all, like ice, she was so uncomfortable and nervous.

Though she'd only been waiting for Blake for fifteen minutes, every one of those minutes had seemed an eternity, giving her ample time to question their relationship even more.

What if he didn't show up? What would that mean? Would their relationship be over? Just like that?

And if he did show, could she really manage to act like they were only friends? Could she minimize her smile? Rein in her feelings?

"Would you prefer herbal or regular tea?" the waiter asked with a slight bow.

"Herbal is fine."

"Actually, sir, I'd like a strong Earl Grey if you wouldn't mind," a voice chimed in from behind her. "Haven't had a decent cup all day. Quite possibly all week."

Oh, that unmistakable accent.

Sam watched as women's heads turned instantly at nearby tables to get a glimpse of the man behind the alluring inflection. Even though some of the ladies were with other men, it didn't appear to matter. Their reaction was involuntary, out of their control. So was the way their eyes danced delightfully, and the way a slight coquettish smile suddenly tugged at their lips.

Some things never change, Sam thought with a sense

of déjà vu. A prideful sort of grin crossed her face as she turned to look at him too.

Whether her friend or lover, she had to admit, he was a dashing sight. No denying that. His tailored black suit fit his muscular physique impeccably, his claret-colored tie knotted neatly at his neck. In fact, his attire was the perfect complement to hers. How did he do that? How could he have known?

Yet the most striking thing about him were his eyes, the way he looked at her. Eyes that glimmered as he took her in, making her feel as if she were the most special woman in the restaurant, the *only* woman in the room. Whether he truly felt that way or not, he could certainly give a female that impression.

From the looks of things, he'd evidently left his wool topcoat with coat check, but he carried a wrapped present in one of his hands. That was curious, Sam thought, since they'd said they weren't exchanging presents, agreeing that their night out would be the best gift yet. Not that she had adhered to that rule either; she had a couple of presents waiting for him under her tree.

But this one was probably for Emma, she surmised as he set the gift on the table, and brushed her cheek lightly with his lips before sitting down at the table.

Was it just a friendly kiss?

She wondered for a moment, but then resisted the temptation to resort to more fretting. The only thing she wanted to think about at the moment was Blake. He was finally here, taking her breath away, looking fantastic.

". . . fantastic,' he said, uttering her exact thoughts as his eyes scanned her face.

He reached across the table and covered her hand with

his, both his compliment and the familiar feel of him causing her to blush, infusing her with warmth.

"It's been just a few days, but I feel like I haven't seen you forever." He squeezed her hand gently.

She tried to steady her thoughts. "Like old friends meeting up again, huh?"

A slight shadow etched his face. "Friends?"

"No," she blurted. *Oh, she was botching this already!* "I just mean, well . . . So you had a busy day?"

He shook his head, his eyes gleaming and steady on her. "Doesn't matter." He dismissed their hours apart. "It's all better now."

The waiter appeared just then, interrupting Blake's burning gaze and the touch of his hand on hers. They both sat back and watched as the waiter placed white porcelain teacups rimmed in gold on either side of the glowing crystal candleholder.

"We'll need a minute," Blake told him, winking.

Winking?

"Take all the time you need, sir." The waiter smiled smugly before scurrying away.

"How's Emma?" He turned back to her, making her quickly forget about the strange exchange.

"Great," she said her hand busy stirring sugar into her tea, already missing his touch. "She had her first bite of carrots today."

"Orange and pureed?" He crinkled his nose.

She nodded. "My reaction exactly."

He sipped his dark tea. "And I hear she sat up?" he asked. His grin was as proud as any daddy's.

"All on her own," she said, trying not to think about the fact that he'd had time to call her aunt yesterday but not her . . . and that all of his questions so far had been about Emma.

But then—would any other man ever care, ever feel like he did about the baby girl? Shouldn't she just be happy he loved Emma so much? As much as she did?

"Is that for Emma?" She nodded at the gift, bracing herself. Hopefully he wouldn't say he brought it tonight because he couldn't make it to see her or Emma on Christmas morning.

"Not exactly." He patted the box.

"Oh . . ." She sat still for a moment.

"For Aunt Maria and Uncle Dom?"

He shook his head again, pursing his lips. "No."

"The waiter?" she teased. "You two seemed fairly friendly a moment ago."

He laughed. "Actually, that would also be a 'no.' "

"Well, I suppose that leaves only me." She tilted her head in mock contemplation. "But then, how can that be since we said we weren't buying presents for one another?"

"Hmm, did we say that? Must have slipped my mind completely." He smiled, sliding the beautifully wrapped box across the ivory tablecloth. "So now that it's here, I suppose you may as well open it."

She'd just gotten over feeling conspicuous. And now he wanted her to open a present? She leaned forward, speaking in a hushed tone. *"Now?* In DeAngelo's?"

He leaned forward, too, the petal-fresh scent of the candle wafting between them. The fervor of his gaze . . . the sheer nearness of him . . . created a warmth so intense within her she knew it couldn't be coming from the candle's light.

Did he feel it, too? This ardor that felt like more than "just friends?"

"Yes, *now* if you don't mind. I don't know about you—but the suspense is killing me."

A rush of feelings swelled up inside of her, causing a giddy-sounding giggle to escape. He was too charming. Too adorable. Too easy to love. "You're impossible."

His roguish grin surfaced. "One of my more endearing traits, don't you think?"

She stared at the gift for a moment not knowing what to think. He'd dismissed the waiter for the time being. Ordering dinner hadn't even been mentioned yet. What else *was* there to do but unwrap the present?

With a tremor of excitement and a twinge of apprehension, she slipped the golden ribbon from around the box. Tearing at the matching foil paper, a familiar salmon color appeared.

"From Chausseures?" She smiled.

He nodded. "Go ahead. Open it. Nothing will jump out at you."

Delicately, she opened the box. Wrapped inside the salmon-colored tissue appeared another familiar sight.

"Oh, Blake!" she exclaimed. "These are the shoes!"

Twilight Tango. The shoes they'd both admired the first day they met.

"May I?" He lifted the heels from the box and before she knew it he was at her feet in the middle of DeAngelo's, removing her every day heels and replacing them with the strappy dancing shoes.

Then he got to his feet and beamed at her. "May I have this dance?"

The moment was so perfect that for once in her life

she didn't care who was watching. She rose to meet him, taking his offered hand, letting her heart lead the way.

Settling into his arms on the small dance floor, she looked up at him, hoping he could see the love in her eyes. "I can't believe you remembered," she whispered, as the music guided their steps.

"I've never forgotten, Sam." He pulled her closer. "I've never forgotten the first moment I met you. I thought you were surely an angel. So beautiful. And heavenly. I felt completely befuddled. Baffled, daffy. Saying such inane things. Rambling on and on. Tripping over my own tongue. So very nervous." He paused and smiled at her. "Not unlike I am right this minute, I suppose."

Blake nervous? It seemed almost paradoxical.

"Why would you be nervous?"

"Sam . . . I want to dance with you."

"We are dancing, Blake. And it's wonderful. You couldn't have given me a more perfect gift."

"Not just for now, Sam. I want to dance with you for always."

"For always?" Her heart bubbled up making her breathless.

"Sam . . . I drove up to Philadelphia the other day. I drove up to see your father."

Her feet stopped moving to music. She pulled her head back, searching the Englishman's eyes. "My father? That's where you were this week? You went to see my dad?"

"Yes, and I'm sorry I didn't call. I started to a dozen times. But I was afraid you'd guess I was out of the area. Or that I'd get carried away and blurt out my surprise accidentally."

His surprise?

Her eyes widened. Did he mean that—? Could she hope that—?

"Your mother was there, too, by the way. At your father's. She'd been there for a week before I arrived. They both send their love and will come visit after their Christmas trip to Jamaica."

Now her mouth hung wide, too. "My father? *And* my mother? Christmas in Jamaica?"

He nodded. "That's why I was late. I had brunch with them this morning. They were full of stories about you. I was totally captivated and lost all track of time."

She would've been more flattered if she wasn't totally caught off guard. "My mother and father are staying together?"

"Well, they *are* married, darling."

"I know . . . it's just so incredible."

"Anyway . . . being the proper gentleman that I am, I wanted to do the proper thing. So I went to ask your father for your hand in marriage. He said 'yes,' Sam. I hope you'll say 'yes' too."

His eyes searched hers and for a moment he looked less like the worldly man he was and more like an unsure adolescent boy asking a girl out for the very first time.

"Sam, will you marry me?" He gazed at her. "I love you so much." His hand pressed fervently on the small of her back, urging her closer to the love they could share together.

"You love *me*?" Her heart was racing, making her feel lightheaded. Could he really be saying what she'd dreamed so often of hearing?

He laughed. "Love you? I'm insane about you. I'd do anything for you, Sam. Anything to make you happy."

Tears pricked at her eyes, happiness overwhelming her. Was it really possible? Could she truly have both the people she loved in her life?

"And here, I thought, well . . . I always knew you loved Emma."

"Of course I love the princess, and I'm ready for the pitter-patter of more little feet. I truly am. After we adopt Emma, there's nothing I'd like better than to start our own brood of six little tykes in the next year or so."

"Six? Seven with Emma?" The number staggered her as much as his admission.

"All right then. Four."

She bit her lip. "I'd always hoped Emma would have a brother or sister. Possibly one of each . . ."

"Okay, three of those little creatures then," he said, flustered. "It's your call, darling. We'll have as many or as few as you like. The point is, I don't want to live without you, Sam."

He looked straight at her, waiting for a reply. But she was so stunned, happily stunned, that she couldn't find her voice for a moment. She simply stood there staring at him with a smile so wide it felt as if her mouth might never close again.

"Well, love—say something. Are you going to make me ask you again? Because I will, you know." He gave her one of his heart-stopping lopsided grins.

"I say 'yes,' Blake, oh, yes. I love you, too. And I've wanted to tell you for so long. But I was afraid you'd feel trapped and be too nice to say anything."

"Trapped?" He rocked back, astonished. "Sam, I want to spend all the years of my life with you. I want to dance with you. Watch sunsets with you. Go fishing with you . . ."

"Fishing?" It was her turn to be taken back. "Um . . . I really don't like fishing."

He chuckled as his arm pulled her close to him. "Darling, believe me, you like fishing. You just don't know you like fishing."

"No, Blake," she stood her ground. "I know. I don't like fishing. But you can feel free to go anytime. I won't feel badly, I promise."

"But, my bride to be, then you'd miss out on everything."

She laughed. "Like worms, mosquitoes and smelly lake water?"

"Not exactly." He kissed her softly on her forehead, and gently laid her head to his shoulder. "More like a rowboat out in the middle of a sun-kissed lake," he whispered into her ear seductively. "With no one else around. A blanket on the grassy bank. And a picnic with all of your favorites . . . strawberries dipped in chocolate . . . gourmet cheeses. Time to lavish in the sun, talk, hold each other while the rest of the world is far, far away."

"It sounds perfect," she whispered back, his description leaving her breathless.

"Of course it does. After all," he pressed her close, "I know what women like."

"Women?" Her head shot up. She quirked an eyebrow at him.

"Correction," he smiled at her lovingly. "Woman. My woman . . . the only woman I'll ever love . . ." he told her, his voice low, his eyes passionate.

For a moment, Sam couldn't hear the music swelling around them. The only sound she heard was Blake's words. Echoing in her head. Filling her heart as he pulled her into his arms, sealing his vow of love with the warm, gentle promise of his kiss.

Epilogue

"I think she likes the wrapping paper better than my present," Blake leaned over and spoke quietly into Sam's ear.

His head propped up on one arm, his other arm around her waist, they lay on Sam's family room floor just a few feet from Emma. Dressed in a red and green sleeper with a reindeer appliqué, the baby girl's rosy cheeks glowed. She looked every bit the picture of Christmas morning—especially with all the colorful scraps of torn wrapping paper and discarded bows dotting the carpet around her.

Catching hold of a shiny silver piece of foil paper, she waved it eagerly in the air. Blake and Sam looked on, watching her every move with wonder.

"Well, she is a bit young for a rocking horse," Sam answered, her skin still tingling where Blake's lips had brushed against her neck.

"True. But I knew her mum would appreciate the fine craftsmanship of the piece." He squeezed her waist. "Besides, sorry to say, our little girl will grow up in a flash. So fast, she'll be rocking away before we know it."

"It really is a beautiful rocking horse, Blake. And you're right." She nestled up against him, wanting him to know how grateful she felt. "I do appreciate it. Anyway, I guess I should just be glad you didn't come home with the real thing," she teased. "I can't imagine taking care of a pony." She chuckled.

As soon as the words left her mouth, she felt his hand loosen around her waist. She turned to look at him, but his eyes darted this way and that. Every way, but her way.

She laughed. "Oh my gosh! You did think about it? You almost bought Em a pony, didn't you?"

"Actually, I did happen to run into a fellow whose mare is birthing in the spring."

Sam cocked an eyebrow. "Ran into?"

"Came across . . ." He shrugged off the semantics.

"Came across?"

"Through my inquiries with directory assistance," he admitted.

She sat up abruptly, trying to appear serious. But hard as she tried, she couldn't hide her amusement. A smile lit up her face as she admonished him. "Blake, you're going to spoil her."

He cocked his head at her. "Yes, love." He sighed. "I probably will. Probably will spoil her mum too." A slow impish grin began to form on his lips. "Don't hold it against me?"

He sat up then, scooping his hand under her hair, pulling her toward him. His first kiss was light, teasing. His second was more ardent, pressing. Telltale of a passion she knew they would share for years to come.

"I'll try not to," she said breathlessly when their lips finally parted.

Emma squealed out loud just then, and they both turned at the delighted sound of her. Much to their amazement, it wasn't a piece of paper or ribbon the baby was so gleeful about. Instead, she seemed happy with herself. She was, after all, sitting up.

"Blake!" Sam exclaimed in a hushed voice.

"I know, love!" His eyes were wide.

Both sat perfectly still hoping not to disturb Emma's major feat.

"Where's the—?" Sam didn't even have to finish her sentence. Both their sets of eyes scoured the messy room for the video camera.

"I think it's—" He nodded in the direction of the low coffee table sitting in front of the couch, covered with remnants of their early morning gift exchange.

"Under the poncho?" She eyed a bit of silver gleaming from under the hand-knit cloak he'd had made for her.

He nodded again.

She was closest to the table and tried to move discreetly, leaning over, pushing away the poncho to get to the video camera.

"I think she's starting to topple," Blake exclaimed, scooting over to catch Emma in his arms.

The camera jiggled as Sam quickly brought it up to her eyes catching flashes of the light morning snow coming down outside the window . . . and glimpses of gifts— books, baby clothes and toys strewn around the room.

It was all so plentiful. All so much. An amazing, heart-warming sight.

And yet, as she steadied the camera in her hands, and

the image of Blake and Emma came in to the viewfinder, her heart absolutely overflowed.

Who needed Christmas presents? She thought focusing on their smiling faces. She had everything she could ever possibly want right in front of her eyes.